Goddess Girls

PANDORA THE CURIOUS

READ ALL THE BOOKS IN THE GODDESS GIRLS SERIES

Athena the Brain

Persephone the Phony

Aphrodite the Beauty

Artemis the Brave

Athena the Wise

Aphrodite the Diva

Artemis the Loyal

Medusa the Mean

Goddess Girls Super Special:

The Girl Games

COMING SOON:

Pheme the Gossip

Persephone the Daring

Goddess Girls

PANDORA THE CURIOUS

JOAN HOLUB & SUZANNE WILLIAMS

Aladdin

NEW YORK LONDON TORONTO SYDNEY NEW DELHI

ALADDIN

An imprint of Simon & Schuster Children's Publishing Division

1230 Avenue of the Americas, New York, NY 10020

First Aladdin paperback edition December 2012

Also available in an Aladdin hardcover edition.

For information about special discounts for bulk purchases, please contact Simon & Schuster Special Sales at 1-866-506-1949 or business@simonandschuster.com.

The Simon & Schuster Speakers Bureau can bring authors to your live event. For more information or to book an event contact the Simon & Schuster Speakers Bureau at 1-866-248-3049 or visit our website at www.simonspeakers.com.

Designed by Karin Paprocki

The text of this book was set in Baskerville Handcut Regular.

Manufactured in the United States of America 0316 OFF

6 8 10 9 7

Library of Congress Control Number 2012942889

ISBN 978-1-4424-4935-0 (pbk)

ISBN 978-1-4424-5975-5 (hc)

ISBN 978-1-4424-4936-7 (eBook)

For our mega-fantastic fans:

Lilly W., Lynda Jane R., Idil B., Liya C.,
Mona P., Maya O., Jae S., Ariel C., Jessica Q.,
Lily-Ann S., Vivian L., Joei C., Lilith W., Echo S.,
Ryanna L., Mikki W., Kate M., Bethany V., Ally D.,
Rebecca Z., Rachel Z., Sarah M., Fres GG Club,
Jocelyn Skye M., Katya B., Zoya B., Kayla S., James A.,
Nick R., Kevin M., Emily May A., Caitlin A.,
Sofia W., Justine Y., Chelsea B., Lorelei T., Nikki L.,
Samantha G., Loren A., Mariane D., Lana W.,
Sarah P., Martha P., Pat D., Zoe M., Denise D.,
Ashley V.L.N., Monet E., Kat G., Alex G.,
Makayla H., MacKenzie W., Maddie T.,
Juliette M., Lene R., Kashara B.,Monica B.,
Rachel K., Briana S., Taylor F., Caitlin F.

–J. H. and S. W.

CONTENTS

1 Mystery Box

PANDORA WAS WALKING DOWN THE HALL TO her favorite class—Science-ology—when she spotted something so interesting that it made her pale blue eyes go wide.

"Ooh!" she breathed. She elbowed Athena, the goddessgirl beside her. Then she pointed the tip of her cream-colored Science-ology textscroll at someone

coming toward them. "See that new Titan boy?"

"You mean Epimetheus?" Athena asked. "What about him?"

Black-haired with gray-green eyes, the Titan godboy and his brother Prometheus had only been attending Mount Olympus Academy for a couple of weeks.

"Don't you see that box he's holding?" Pandora couldn't take her eyes off it. It glowed and twitched in Epimetheus's hands. And interesting sounds were coming from it. Like mouse squeaks, salpinx trumpets, and tiger growls all mixed together. "What do you think is in it?" she asked as they paused at the hall fountain.

Athena shrugged. "Hard to say."

Epimetheus had stopped at his locker nearby. Pandora kept an eye on him and his box as she and Athena took turns sipping the glittering nectar that arced from the fountain's spout.

When the immortal godboys and goddessgirls at Mount Olympus Academy drank nectar, it caused their skin to shimmer. It had no effect on Pandora's skin, though. Because she was mortal. One of the few mortals Principal Zeus had invited to go to school here at MOA.

Athena was eyeing the box now too as she straightened from the fountain. "Well, maybe it's—" she started to say.

"Could it be an ancient jewelry box or something?" Pandora interrupted, unable to wait for Athena to finish. The box was about the right size for that. "Ooh! Maybe there's a bracelet in it? Or something magical? Like a teeny genie?"

"A bracelet or a genie wouldn't make those weird noises, though," said Athena. Holding her long wavy brown hair back with one hand, she took another quick sip of nectar from the fountain.

Afterward her golden skin shimmered a little more brightly. Because, unlike Pandora, Athena was a goddessgirl. She was also the brainiest student at school. She and Pandora were roommates, sharing a room in the girls' dorm upstairs on MOA's fourth floor.

"C'mon. Let's get to class," Athena said.

But Pandora grabbed her arm, stopping her. "Wait! Aren't you dying of curiosity? *I* am."

Athena faked a look of shock. "No!" she gasped. "You? Curious? Really?"

Pandora grinned. She had a reputation for being more curious than practically anyone else at the Academy. In fact, as a sign of her curious nature, her blue and gold bangs were shaped in the form of question marks. But what was wrong with being curious? Nothing, in her opinion!

"Well, I think somebody should ask him what's in that

box, don't you?" asked Pandora. "I mean, who knows what he might have in there? It could even be something dangerous!"

Without waiting for Athena's reply, Pandora took a step in Epimetheus's direction. But before she could take another step, someone behind her called out in a mean voice.

"Hey! Dork-i-metheus!" It was Kydoimos. He and his godboy pal Makhai pushed past Pandora and Athena. Kydoimos was laughing so hard at his own joke that he didn't seem to notice when his shoulder bumped Athena. One of the three textscrolls she was holding went flying.

It hit the floor by Pandora's sandaled feet. She stooped to pick it up and then handed it back to Athena.

"Aren't you even going to say 'Excuse me'?" she called after the boys. But they didn't hear. They were too busy making a beeline for Epimetheus.

When it came to Titans, the godboys at MOA were always itching to start trouble. In some ways that was understandable. The Titans had fought a war against the most powerful and important god at the Academy—Principal Zeus. They'd tried to keep him from becoming King of the Gods and Ruler of the Heavens.

Zeus had defeated them, of course. And the war was long past now. Still, a lot of distrust remained.

Everyone knew that Epimetheus and Prometheus were the sons of Iapetus, a Titan god who had battled Zeus. So most of the students, Pandora included, couldn't help wondering why Zeus had invited the sons of his enemy to go to school here. But he must have had his reasons.

So shouldn't they give these Titans a chance? *What if the situation were reversed?* she wondered. If one of MOA's godboys got sent to a Titan school, wouldn't they want to be treated with kindness?

"Whatcha got in the box, Dork-i-metheus?" Kydoimos asked Epimetheus before Pandora could ask him herself. Except she wouldn't have called him a dork, of course. Kydoimos really acted like a bully sometimes. Same went for Makhai.

Epimetheus didn't answer. He only clutched his mysterious box tighter and shut his locker. Then he headed off for class.

Excited curiosity bubbled in Pandora. Since Epimetheus was in Science-ology next too, he was going the same way she and Athena were. Maybe she could get a better look at the box in class.

As Pandora and Athena fell into step behind Epimetheus, Makhai sneaked up next to him. In a flash Makhai snatched the box away.

"No!" Looking freaked out, Epimetheus made a wild grab for it.

"Over here!" yelled Kydoimos, laughing. Running backward down the hall, he went long. His arms were raised like he was going out for a pass. Other students leaped aside in a hurry to get out of his way.

Makhai tossed the box toward him. Everyone watched it sail overhead in a high arc, nearly brushing the domed ceiling. The inside of the dome was covered with paintings that illustrated the glorious exploits of the gods and goddesses, including their long-ago battle with the Titans.

Pandora glimpsed Poseidon, the tall, blond godboy of the sea. His turquoise eyes had narrowed fiercely when they'd landed on the battle paintings. Then they darted to the mystery box. It had overshot and was hurtling past Kydoimos. Pandora gasped, afraid the box would smash on the marble-tiled floor.

But Poseidon saved the day, leaping to catch it in one hand.

What a hero! thought Pandora, sighing with admiration. Like numerous other girls at MOA, she'd been crushing on the mega-cute Poseidon for years.

Epimetheus lunged for him. "Give it back! That box could be dangerous!"

Dangerous? Pandora's eyes rounded in dismay. Hadn't she expressed that concern to Athena just minutes ago? Only, Pandora hadn't really expected to be right!

Looking startled, Poseidon shot a worried glance at the box, then quickly tossed it away. It fell into the hands of another godboy named Apollo. He looked startled too, and tossed it to Ares, the godboy of war.

After that it was tossed from hand to hand as if it were a hot potato. Since nothing bad happened as a result, the tossing soon turned into a boisterous game of Keep Away.

"Epimetheus looks upset," Athena murmured.

"I know. I feel kind of sorry for him, don't you?" said Pandora.

Athena nodded. "If everyone stops watching, maybe the boys will quit teasing him. C'mon." She tugged Pandora's arm, hinting that they should leave.

But Pandora had her eyes glued to that box. She just *had* to know what was in it!

The box gleamed in the rays of sunlight drifting in through the windows, looking like a rectangular golden sun. However, when Athena kept tugging at her arm, Pandora reluctantly went. Still, she kept watching the game over her shoulder.

Every time the box fell into a new set of hands, Epimetheus veered in a new direction. He skidded back and forth across the hall, desperately trying to retrieve the box.

Suddenly one of the boys' throws went wild. Pandora

lost sight of Epimetheus's box as the entire group of boys made a rambunctious leap all at once. Hands reached. There were shouts and whoops of laughter. The box tumbled and was knocked about in the mass attempt to grab it.

Amid the frenzy Pandora and Athena got separated in the crowded hallway. Pandora was pushed into a corner at the end of a row of lockers. Going up on tiptoe, she was looking for Athena, when, unexpectedly, the mysterious box dropped . . .

right

into

her

hands.

Plunk!

2
Ditz

PANDORA STARED AT THE BOX, ALMOST HYPNOtized by its magnificence. And it had fallen right into her lap—er, hands. How lucky could she get?

"Ye gods!" she whispered. It was even more amazing up close than it had been at a distance. It was about ten inches long and was decorated on all sides with carved swirls. The top was inlaid with a circlet of gleaming amethyst jewels.

There was also tiny lettering, but it was in some strange language she couldn't read. Still, as she stared at the words, they began to somehow make more sense to her. She could almost read them. Almost, but not quite. Maybe if she had more time.

She looked up as she heard Epimetheus yell, "Where's my box?"

"I don't have it!" she heard several godboys say. The boys around her were all way taller than she was, and at the moment their backs were to her. So for now no one realized she had the box.

Cradling it in one arm, she reached with her free hand to touch the box's shiny golden clasp. Unfortunately, she could see that it was locked. She ran a fingertip over it, and then pushed on the lock ever so slightly.

Click! To her surprise it separated in the middle, its two halves parting. Her pale blue eyes glittered with interest.

Would there be something awesome inside? This might be her only chance to find out. She knew the box wasn't hers to open, but she had to see if she'd guessed right!

Still, her hand wavered as she reached to open the box. Epimetheus had warned the boys that it could be dangerous. Yet nothing had happened when they'd tossed it around. And the lock had sprung easily at her touch.

It was almost as if the box *wanted* her to look inside it. What could be the harm in taking one little peek?

In an instant Pandora's curiosity overcame her. She opened the lid, just a bit. As she did, an ominous sound like the rumble of gathering storm clouds roared forth. Then came a flash of lightning in the hall. And the crash of thunder.

All around her, students were ducking and look-

ing around anxiously. It wasn't every day that thunder crashed *inside* the school.

Did it mean Principal Zeus was coming? He'd thrown thunderbolts around before, though usually outside. She listened, but didn't hear his booming voice or the stomp of his sandals.

So Pandora didn't duck or run. She saw no reason to. The box held her spellbound. In one smooth swing she lifted its lid all the way open. And then she frowned in surprise.

What was this? *Glass balls?*

She quickly counted ten of them in the box. Each glowing ball was a different color and was about two inches in diameter. As she held the box, they all sparkled and trembled gently. But the weird sounds she'd heard earlier were silent now.

Then some of the balls began to rise and float away.

Pandora gasped. They weren't made of glass at all. They were bubbles!

She silently named their colors as they escaped. *Blue, purple, green . . .*

"Pandora has it!" someone yelled.

She looked up, startled to have been spotted. More bubbles drifted out of the box. *Orange, bronze, pink . . .*

"No-o-o!" she heard Epimetheus shout. His voice seemed far away.

The crowd parted. As if in slow motion he began to stumble toward her. Meanwhile, three more bubbles escaped. *Red, turquoise, chartreuse . . .*

Before the tenth bubble—a bright golden yellow one—could escape, Epimetheus caught up to her. Snatching the box from her grasp, he slammed the lid down so fast, it almost caught her fingers. *Snap!* Just like an alligator's jaws.

"Hey! Be careful, will you?" Pandora snapped back at him. The top of her head only reached to his shoulder. But then, she was dainty, shorter than almost everyone else in her grade.

Epimetheus bent his head. His gray-green eyes peered closely at her, and he studied her face with a concerned expression. "Are you okay?"

"Uh-huh. Why?" She gazed up at him, puzzled. Other boys had crowded around behind him, all watching to see what would happen.

Epimetheus tuned them out, his attention only on her. "No reason," he said. "But, I mean, you opened the box."

"Yeah, so?" Did this boy really think bubbles were dangerous?

He heaved a rather annoyed sigh. "Well? Was there anything *in* the box?"

She sent him a confused look. “It’s your box. Don’t you know?” If he hadn’t put those bubbles in there, who had? Besides, hadn’t he seen them escaping a second ago?

Ping! Ping! The lyrebell rang, signaling that the next class period was about to begin. Other students lost interest in the show and started to leave. Game over.

Athena finally managed to push her way through the crowd to Pandora’s side. “Are you okay?” she asked, echoing Epimetheus’s question.

Pandora nodded. Ignoring Athena, Epimetheus stared from the box to Pandora and back again. “This box is impossible to open!” he declared.

“Oh, really?” said Pandora, arching an eyebrow. “Then how did I open it?”

“Good question. How *did* you?” Epimetheus mumbled as he examined the box carefully from all angles. To her surprise, Pandora saw that it had locked itself tight again.

Pandora shrugged. "I don't know. I barely touched it."

Athena smiled brightly. "Well, no harm done, then."

Epimetheus frowned at her. "I'm not so sure about that."

Honestly! thought Pandora. What was wrong with this annoying Titan? Couldn't he see that his precious box was fine? Of course, all but one of its bubbles were gone now. But since he didn't even seem to know what had been inside, she decided not to tell him. Why risk making him mad?

While Athena asked him what he'd meant by what he'd just said, Pandora's eyes tracked the nine escaped bubbles. *Why wasn't anyone else looking at them?* she wondered. Hadn't they noticed?

Some of the bubbles had risen high in the air by now.

Others were aimlessly drifting down the hall. A few floated out an open window.

Pandora ducked as a bubble abruptly did a nose-dive and headed straight at her. It was the blue one. She automatically thumped it away with a finger before it could touch her cheek. It ricocheted over and bumped Athena's forehead instead.

"Ditz," a soft voice whispered. *Pop!* The bubble disappeared.

"Who are you calling a 'ditz'?" Pandora demanded.

Athena and Epimetheus both looked at her blankly. "What?" they asked at the same time.

"You didn't hear . . ." Her words faded uncertainly. Maybe she'd only imagined someone saying "Ditz." After all, the hall was still pretty noisy with everyone scurrying to class.

Ping! Ping! Ping!

When the final bell rang, Athena reached around Epimetheus and grabbed Pandora's hand. "Scuse us," she said. Then she let out a very un-Athena-like giggle. "Gotta run!"

With that the two girls rushed down the hall to Science-ology. Once inside the classroom Pandora took her usual seat front row center. Athena sat behind her.

Epimetheus didn't arrive till long after the bell. Lucky for him the teacher was late too. He didn't have the box with him anymore, and Pandora wondered what he'd done with it.

Her eyes followed him as he went to sit by his brother, Prometheus, one row over in the last desk. Rumor had it that Prometheus had been held back a year at their previous school. Since Epimetheus was a year younger than him, that's how the two boys had wound up in the same grade.

The two Titan brothers put their heads together now, whispering. As they talked, Epimetheus kept shooting Pandora worried, suspicious glances. It was like just because she'd opened his dumb box, he now expected her to grow nine heads or something. Hey, she wasn't Ms. Hydra from the front office, who actually *did* have nine heads!

Well, so what if he thought she was weird? Because she thought *he* was the weird one. Who carried around a growling, thundering box with bubbles inside it?

She looked away when he suddenly caught her eye. She supposed he was sort of cute. All the other girls seemed to think so, anyway. But her crush was Poseidon.

Her eyes cut in his direction. He was in his usual seat on the other side of the aisle, right behind Apollo. Even from here she could see that Poseidon's mouth was set in its usual cocky grin. His turquoise skin shimmered, and his blond hair was perfectly styled as always.

As she watched, he twirled his trident, which looked like a pitchfork, only cooler, above his head like a baton a few times. Then he stabbed its pointy prongs down into the floor beside his desk. He did that at the beginning of every class.

"Stay," he commanded. Obediently it stood upright.

Pandora rested her chin on one hand, gazing at him in admiration. He was so awesome! And he knew it. Still, that was okay with her. How could someone so epically awesome *not* know it?

She was distracted from her study of him when Principal Zeus himself suddenly walked into the room. At seven feet tall with bulging muscles, wild red hair, and piercing blue eyes, he was a pretty intimidating sight.

Immediately everyone got quiet, the same questions in their eyes. Why was the principal here? Where was their teacher, Muse Urania?

"GOOD MORNING, CLASS!" Zeus hailed them in his usual booming voice. "You're probably wondering where your teacher is. Well, she had to rush down to Greece to do some research with the illustrious astronomer Hipparchus. He's got some odd notion that the Earth isn't the center of the universe.

"Anyhoo, as you'll no doubt be thrilled to know, I'm stepping in as a substitute teacher for this entire week!" Spreading his powerful arms wide, he stood there like he was waiting for applause.

Athena–she was his daughter–started clapping. This was a good idea, and since no one ever wanted to be on Zeus's bad side, everyone else quickly joined in.

Zeus smiled broadly and went to stand behind the teacher's desk. There he briefly studied Muse Urania's lesson planscroll. "Looks like today's lesson is, um . . ." He stopped, frowning at what he'd read.

Apparently Muse Urania's plan for today didn't exactly thrill him. Sighing, he rolled up the lesson plan-scroll and shoved it aside. Everyone waited as he came around and sat on the front edge of the teacher's desk. He stroked his red beard thoughtfully for a moment.

A few seconds later his eyes lit up and he rubbed his hands together craftily. Tiny sparks of electricity shot out from between his palms in every direction. This often happened when Zeus was around, so no one panicked.

A random spark landed on Pandora's desk, causing a tiny flame to burn the corner of her textscroll. She casually slipped off her sandal, used it to smack the cinder out, and then put her sandal back on.

Finally Zeus spoke. "As you all know, I'm King of the Gods and Ruler of the Heavens. So I can do what I like. And I *like* competition. So I propose that we skip today's

astronomy lesson and plan a science fair instead. The kind with science projects that win prizes. What do you say?"

Everyone looked at everyone else. Grins formed and widened. Textscrolls snapped shut. Some of the godboys punched fists into the air. "Yeah!"

Pandora had to admit it. Zeus had good ideas.

He smiled at their enthusiasm, then went on. "You can choose a project in any of the sciences, and—"

Pandora's hand shot high into the air before he could finish. The whole class groaned. She knew it was because she was always interrupting. Still, she couldn't help herself.

And anyway, she figured that half the time others were actually glad she asked questions. Because they often wanted to know the answers to the very questions she asked. Only they were too shy to voice the questions themselves. Or when it came to querying Zeus, maybe they were too *nervous* to ask!

When he called on her, a question burst from her lips. "What will the prizes be?"

Zeus brightened at this question. It was no secret that he was like a little kid when it came to contests and prizes. "There'll be three prizes in all," he explained. "Three *amazing* prizes for first, second, and third places."

He went on, but Pandora didn't even hear. As usual her mind was already whirling with new questions. She raised her hand again.

The toe of one of Zeus's golden sandals tapped the floor. For some reason his bushy red brows bunched up like he was impatient or annoyed. Probably it was only because being principal and King of the Gods, et cetera, meant he had a lot on his mind, she decided.

"Who will judge the fair?" she asked when he finally called on her.

"Well, I was just about to tell you that," Zeus said, sounding a little bit testy. "I will invite three of the greatest mortal scientists on Earth as judges. Hippocrates, Aristotle, and Pythagoras."

At this news the whole class buzzed with excitement. These were impressive judges, to be sure.

Pandora looked over her shoulder at Athena, who should have been jumping for joy. Instead she was painting her fingernails and reading *Teen Scrollazine.* Pandora's eyes widened in surprise. Where had her roommate gotten the nail polish and the scrollazine? They weren't the kind of things she normally carried around.

Besides that, she didn't even seem to be listening to her dad. Talk about weird! Athena loved science. In fact, she'd recently gotten permission to switch from Beauty-ology to Science-ology third period.

"Did you hear what Zeus said?" Pandora whispered to her. "Pythagoras is going to be a judge for the science fair."

Athena glanced up from her task, a look of blank confusion in her blue-gray eyes. "Pythaga-who?"

3
Pick Me!

"PYTHAGORAS," PANDORA REPEATED.

Athena shrugged and blew on her fingernails. She darted a look at Zeus to be sure he hadn't noticed what she was doing.

"Where did you get the nail polish?" Pandora whispered.

"Borrowed it from Iris." Athena held up her fingers

so that Pandora could admire her handiwork. Although the polish had come from one bottle, it was magical. So the polish on each of Athena's fingernails was a different color. Made sense, since Iris was into rainbows.

Pandora turned to face front as Zeus began speaking again. But she was still wondering what was up with Athena. As her roomie, she knew that the brainy girl was a huge Pythagoras fan.

Other MOA girls pinned pictures of cute animals, cute heroes, or cute godboys on their bulletin boards in their dorm rooms. But Athena had pictures of scientists, inventors, and other brainy types. The biggest picture on her bulletin board was of Pythagoras. He was, like, her idol. How could she possibly have forgotten who he was?

And then there was the nail polish. Pandora had only ever seen Athena wear it once. And that was when

Aphrodite—the goddessgirl of love and beauty—had given her a makeover for a party!

Zeus was explaining the rules of the fair now. "The scientific method is an organized way to find the answer to a question," he told them. "You will all use this method in creating your fair projects."

As each word left his lips, it magically appeared as writing on the scrollboard that hung on the wall behind him at the front of the room. The board took up a third of the wall space and kept rolling up at the top as Zeus spoke. So there was always more blank space to write on at the bottom.

But you had to take notes quickly if you wanted to get everything down. Pandora grabbed a sheet of papyrus and her feather pen, then began scribbling away as more words appeared.

SCIENTIFIC METHOD:

1. QUESTION - WHAT QUESTION WILL YOUR PROJECT ANSWER?

2. RESEARCH - GET INFORMATION.

3. HYPOTHESIS - TRY TO PREDICT THE ANSWER TO YOUR QUESTION.

4. EXPERIMENT - TEST YOUR HYPOTHESIS.

5. ANALYSIS - RECORD WHAT HAPPENED.

6. CONCLUSION - WAS YOUR HYPOTHESIS CORRECT?

After rereading the six steps Pandora thought of another question. She raised her hand again. Only, Zeus didn't seem to notice. He was looking everywhere *except* at her. Strange.

Pandora leaned forward in her chair and waved her arm from side to side. Zeus looked at the floor. So she reached low, waving her arm near her feet to catch his attention. But then he switched his gaze to the ceiling. She stretched her hand high, bouncing in her seat.

He looked left. She waved left. He looked right. She waved right. If she didn't know better, she'd think he was avoiding her!

"Hold your questions for now," Zeus finally told the class. He was looking directly at her.

What? Pandora's hand sank. But her brows rose as high as her question mark bangs. *No questions?* If her questions went unasked, they might get bottled up. She could explode!

"But science is all about questions, isn't it?" she blurted out. "Like 'What if?' 'Why?' 'How?' If we can't ask such questions here in Science-ology, where *can* we ask them?"

Zeus frowned at her. But he also seemed a little

impressed by her reasoning. "True," he admitted. "However, for now I want you each to focus your attention on one question only."

The gold band on his left wrist flashed as he unrolled the scrollboard to the top. He pointed to the first step of the scientific method. "And that's the question your project will answer."

"But–," said Pandora.

Zeus made another announcement before she could finish. "Your projects for the fair will be done in teams. You have ten minutes to choose a partner!"

There was a sudden, mad scramble to pair up. Pandora automatically glanced at Poseidon. With a hopeful glint in her eye, she jumped up and went over to him. "Want to be my partner?" she asked.

"Sorry, no can do," he said, shaking his head. His blond hair flopped cutely over one eye, and she watched him push it back. "I want to win first prize," he went on. "A lunch with all three of the judges would be awesome."

So that's what the grand prize was. She must have missed hearing it when she was talking to Athena. But—wow! She'd like to win that herself.

"Me too," she told him. "I bet we could win it together?" When she was nervous or excited about something, she often turned statements into questions. Half the time she didn't even realize she was doing it.

"Well, no offense," Poseidon said. "But I don't think girls are all that great at science. I think Apollo is my best shot at winning." He looked over at Apollo. "What do you say, bud?"

"Partners it is!" said Apollo. They bumped knuckles.

Pandora's eyes narrowed. She felt like she'd just been issued a challenge. And also like she—well, not just her, *all* girls, really—had just been insulted. Why Poseidon would choose Apollo over her was a mystery. Apollo was the godboy of music, prophecy, and other stuff. But not of science!

If Pandora were an immortal, she'd probably be the goddess of curiosity. And that was something you needed for a project like this. She'd show them. If it was the last thing she did, she was going to beat these two godboys in the science fair! Which meant she'd need a smart partner.

Pandora slipped back into her own seat and turned around to talk to Athena. She was the star of the class. Teamed up, they'd be a shoo-in.

"Hey, roomie. Want to be my partner?" Pandora asked, hoping no one else had already asked her. "With my scientific curiosity plus your brains, we'll win for sure!"

"Oh, gosh, thanks!" Athena giggled. "But–" She looked at a mortal boy named Heracles, who sat across the aisle from her.

He smiled at Pandora apologetically. "Sorry. I already snagged her." He was wearing his usual outlandish lion-skin cape. The lion's jaws fit around his head as a hood. So it almost looked as if Heracles were speaking from out of its mouth! Of course, he was Athena's crush, so it was no wonder she'd agreed to be partners with him.

Disappointed, Pandora gave them a tight smile. "Okay, no problem."

She turned to her left. Iris and another goddessgirl named Antheia had their heads together. Apparently they were already partners too. She looked across the room. Two godboys named Hephaestus and Dionysus had partnered. At the far corner of the room, Makhai and Kydoimos were working together.

Everywhere she turned, pairs. Looked like she was going to be left without a partner. How could that be when this was the one class in which her curiosity was bound to be a huge bonus? Why wasn't everyone trying to snag *her*?

"I don't get it," she murmured under her breath.

"Don't get what?"

She looked up to see Epimetheus standing by her desk. "Nothing," she said, feeling a little embarrassed. He must have noticed that she'd been left out. "It's just that I hate it whenever we pick partners."

She was always picked last–if at all. And she could remember every single time it had happened. Like back in third grade, when they chose sides for javelin ball. *Last.* And earlier this year, when the lineup of flag team members was selected. *Last again.*

If only Pheme or Medusa were in this class. One of

them would partner with her. Unfortunately, many girls chose not to take Science-ology. Which was totally dumb, since it was the most fascinating subject ever, in Pandora's opinion. When it came to science, there were questions to be asked everywhere you looked.

"I'm not a ditz," she informed him, still unsure whether he'd called her that in the hall or not.

"Never said you were," he agreed easily. "I think you're smart."

"Smart? Really?" Did he have her confused with Athena?

"Yeah. Only smart people question things." He shifted from one foot to the other, as if a little nervous. Then he said, "So the reason I came over here is . . . Do you want to partner with Prometheus and me?"

Gratitude welled up in her. But she was cautious. "Are you good at science?" she asked him.

“Are you?” he countered.

“Are you kidding?” She stood so she wouldn’t have to crane her neck so much to look at him. “Curiosity is a gift in the scientific world, you know. You’d be lucky to get me on your team.”

“So is that a yes?” His gray-green eyes sparkled with amusement. Looking into them, Pandora could kind of understand why other girls found him cute. Not that *she* did, of course.

She considered his offer. It wasn’t like she had any choice. It was either partner with the Titans or with the class pet hamster. Which Epimetheus happened to be holding in his palm. He was stroking its fur with his other hand. The hamster seemed to like it, because its big brown eyes had drifted closed.

Everyone knew that Epimetheus liked animals. On his first day at MOA he’d had a huge argument with Heracles about that lion-skin cape he wore. He'd accused Heracles of cruelty for slaying the lion. He'd only dropped his complaint later when he'd learned that that particular lion had been on a rampage, killing mortals on Earth.

"What's up?" Prometheus had come over. He looked back and forth between them, a question in his eyes.

"I asked Pandora to be our partner," Epimetheus admitted.

At this news Prometheus's jaw gaped open so wide that he looked somewhat like the hood of Heracles' lion cape. Only, without a boy's head in his mouth. He frowned. "Bro," he said, shaking his head. "I don't think—"

Epimetheus ignored him. "So what do you say?" he asked her.

"There you go again, acting before you think things through," Prometheus muttered.

Pandora bristled on Epimetheus's behalf. She'd often been accused of acting before thinking things through too, and she hated when people told her that. After shooting Prometheus a defiant glance, she smiled at Epimetheus. "Sure. I'll partner with you."

Her reply made Epimetheus grin. "Awesome!"

"Yeah, well, don't do us any favors," said Prometheus.

But she *was* doing them a favor in a way, she decided. After all, they didn't have many friends. On the other hand Epimetheus hadn't needed to ask her to partner with them, since he had his brother as a partner already. So why had he asked her? Did it have something to do with that whole box business?

She glanced Poseidon's way and saw he was joking around with Apollo. Why couldn't *he* have asked her to be a third partner with him and Apollo? Maybe it had just never occurred to him, like it hadn't to her. At any rate, she'd already said yes to the Titans. So that was that.

She looked back at Epimetheus, only to discover that he'd been studying her closely. Now his eyes flicked from her to Poseidon and back again.

Pandora folded her arms defensively. "Did you only ask me to be partners so you can keep tabs on me? Still worried your box had some weird effect on me just because I opened it?"

"You did *what*?" Prometheus's eyes bugged out. He shot an accusing look at his brother. "You let her—"

"It was an accident," she interrupted, though that wasn't exactly true. She didn't want to get Epimetheus in trouble with his brother.

"How did you open it?" Prometheus asked her. He looked mad.

"It was easy. Want me to show you?" She said this even

though she knew Epimetheus hadn't brought his box to class. Maybe this was her chance to find out what he'd done with it. "Where is it?" she asked innocently.

"Somewhere safe," said Epimetheus.

"Yeah." Prometheus crossed his fingers and the two boys shared a secret look. "So what was in it?" he asked her, in an eager tone of voice.

"Yeah, you never said," Epimetheus hinted.

Godness, hadn't either one of them ever thought of *looking* in their own box! Pandora wondered.

"Bubbles," she informed them. She didn't add that all but one had escaped when she'd opened the box.

The Titans both frowned in disbelief. "If you don't want to tell us, fine," said Epimetheus. Turning away, he went over to put the hamster back into its cage.

Yeah, fine is right, thought Pandora. *If they didn't want to hear the truth, then* whatever*!*

Suddenly Principal Zeus spoke up, drawing everyone's attention. "Have you all got partners?" he asked, looking around the room. Pandora was relieved that she didn't have to raise her hand and say she didn't. She was sure Zeus would be okay with one three-partner group, since there was an odd number of students in the class.

"EXCELLENT!" said Zeus. "Then start discussing project ideas. By class time tomorrow, you should be ready to begin your research."

Pandora's gaze fell on an Earth Science textscroll on Muse Urania's desk, which gave her an idea. "How about if we do some kind of experiment to help mortals?" she suggested to her partners as soon as Epimetheus came back.

"Like what?" he asked. She could tell from the interested expressions on the two boys' faces that both were intrigued by her idea.

"Well, I don't know exactly," she said. "Maybe we

could give them something they need?" But when they couldn't immediately come up with the best thing to give, they brainstormed other ideas too.

Epimetheus wondered about asking the question, "What would happen if animals ruled the Earth?" But they decided that an experiment to test that would be too hard.

Prometheus suggested the question, "Why do MOA godboys think they're so great?" But Pandora and Epimetheus agreed that this question would only cause trouble. They still hadn't come up with a firm project by the time the lyrebell rang.

"What are we going to do?" Pandora asked.

"Let's all keep thinking," Epimetheus said. "We'll come up with something."

Before everyone left class, Zeus tossed out one last bit of news. "The fair will take place at the end of the week—

this coming Friday. Prizes will be awarded the following Monday."

This information had almost the same effect as if he'd tossed a thunderbolt into the middle of the classroom. Everyone began talking, sounding rattled at the short time frame.

When Prometheus headed for the door, Epimetheus hung back to talk to Pandora. "Look, I didn't ask you to partner with us because I wanted to see if the box had any harmful effects on you," he explained. "Well, I guess that was part of the reason. But also I wanted you to know that I do admire your curiosity. I get you."

He got her? He admired her? Pandora didn't think he'd ever noticed her before today.

For a second his admiration sent a happy feeling zinging through her. But then she shook it off. It wasn't that important if Epimetheus *got her.*

She wanted the other students at MOA to *get* her too. Especially Poseidon. When she asked questions, most of them acted like she was as annoying as a gnat. Maybe, just maybe, they'd finally appreciate her curiosity if her team won the fair.

"The only thing is," Epimetheus said, "and don't take this the wrong way, but I really think you should be more careful about sticking your nose into things that don't concern you."

Humph! Pandora huffed. Was he implying she was nosy? Just as she decided she'd likely been insulted, Prometheus called to him from the door. Epimetheus dashed off before she could come up with a snappy retort.

As they left class, Pandora asked Athena, "Do you think I'm nosy? Or only curious?"

"Oh, I don't know," said Athena. "Is there a difference?"

She was talking in a bubbly voice that was quite unlike her normal one.

"Of course there is!" said Pandora. "Nosy is nosy. Like Pheme." She wasn't being mean. It was completely true. Pheme, who was the goddessgirl of gossip, was *very* nosy.

"And curious is curious," Pandora went on. "Like me."

Once they were out in the hall, she spied one of the box bubbles still bobbing along overhead about halfway up to the ceiling. The purple one. She looked around, thinking maybe she would point it out to Epimetheus after all, but she didn't see him anywhere.

"Do you see that bubble up there?" she asked Athena.

Athena looked up, then shook her head. "Nuh-uh." But she was looking way left of where the bubble was.

Before Pandora could point to the purple bubble again, it suddenly drifted lower. It was headed for a girl that was walking toward them. A girl with dark curly hair who was being followed by three dogs. It was Artemis, one of Athena's three best friends.

As Pandora watched, the bubble dive-bombed Artemis. *Pop!* It broke against her cheek.

"Vain," a tiny voice whispered.

"Did you hear that?" Pandora asked Artemis as they all three met up. "Someone said 'Vain.'"

But Artemis ignored Pandora's question completely. Instead she asked anxiously, "Does my hair look okay?"

Huh? Pandora moved her head from side to side, studying Artemis's glossy black hair. She'd caught it up in a cute, simple twist high at the back of her head. Golden bands encircled it as always.

"Looks fine," said Pandora. "Same way it always looks."

"Are you sure? I think I'd better run up to my room to double-check," said Artemis. She turned around and

took off for the stairs that led up to the dorms, her dogs trotting after her.

"Since when is she so concerned about how she looks?" Pandora asked Athena in surprise. Artemis cared less about stuff like that than anyone else she knew!

Athena stuck a finger in her long wavy brown hair and wrapped a curl around it. Her eyes went wide and vacant. "I don't know." She giggled.

Then she frowned at the armload of textscrolls she held. "Ye gods! Why am I lugging all these around? Think I'll park them in my locker. Reading gives me a headache anyway. Ta-ta!"

Pandora's jaw dropped as she watched her go. What was up with that girl? She loved to read! And now Artemis was acting weird too. What was going on?

4
Liverwurst

AS PANDORA STOOD IN THE LUNCH LINE A while later, she spotted Poseidon and Apollo ahead of her. Gazing at her not-so-secret (except maybe to *him*) crush made her forget all about Athena, Artemis, and those bubbles.

Aphrodite had once given her some advice at a dance about how to talk to Poseidon. "Ask him one question," she'd said. "And then listen to his entire answer before you say another word."

So later during the dance Pandora had asked him about his trident. And Aphrodite's advice had worked! Maybe it would work again. Maybe if she asked him something now and waited, they would soon start chatting away. Maybe that would lead to them hanging out. And then that would lead to him crushing on her too. It could happen, right?

Taking a deep breath, Pandora plucked up the courage to try out Aphrodite's advice a second time. "Hey, Poseidon," she said casually. "What are you guys doing for your fair project?"

Then, even though she wanted to ask another question right away, she made herself wait for his answer. It was hard. Very hard. Luckily, neither Poseidon nor Apollo seemed to notice how tightly she was pressing her lips together to keep another word from slipping out.

Tossing his blond hair out of his eyes with a flick of his head, Poseidon smiled at her. Whoa. He had the best smile ever! Not that it was directed at her all that often, unfortunately. But maybe that could change?

"Our scientific question is going to be, 'Which musical instrument is most melodious when played underwater?'" he told her. "Great idea, right?"

"Uh, sure?" she replied hesitantly.

Behind her Pandora heard Epimetheus and his brother snicker. But when she looked at them, they didn't appear to be laughing. Was she imagining things again, or had they actually been laughing at Poseidon's idea? She'd been unsure about his idea herself but hadn't wanted to tell him.

As the eight-armed lunch lady handed Prometheus a plate, he groaned. "Liverwurst roll-ups? I *hate* liver."

"Yeah," Pandora joked. "Liver is the *worst.*"

It made her grin when Epimetheus cracked up. Not many students at MOA gave her credit for having a sense of humor.

When it came to liver, Prometheus *really* didn't have a sense of humor. He rolled his eyes at Pandora. "Ha. Ha." He handed the plate with the liverwurst back to the lunch lady, and she gave him a plate of ambrosia salad instead.

Pandora wasn't a salad person or a liver person, so she got the ambrosia loaf. As Epimetheus got the salad, she noticed that he was staring at her again. "Why do you keep looking at me like that?" she asked as they left the line and walked alongside each other with their trays.

Before Epimetheus could answer, she continued, "Do you like me or something? Because if you like me, you can forget it. Because I already have a crush." She didn't want to hurt his feelings. She just thought it was best to make things clear to him.

"Oh?" The tips of Epimetheus's ears turned red. "Who is it? Poseidon?"

She felt her face grow warm. How had he guessed? "Maybe."

"Why do you like him?" he asked. He waited patiently for her answer. Which surprised her, because his brother had said he usually acted before thinking things through. She sort of wished he *would* rush on, because his silence made her uncomfortable.

"I just do," she said at last.

"Give me one reason," he insisted.

"Um. He's epically good at twirling his trident?"

Epimetheus made a face. "What kind of dumb reason is that?"

Just then Makhai walked by them with his tray. "Aw,

how sweet. *Dork*-i-metheus and Pan*dork*a sittin' in a tree. *K-I-S-S-I-N-G.*"

Kydoimos and another godboy named Hades were right behind him. Kydoimos made a kissy sound. He and Makhai laughed. But Epimetheus coolly ignored them.

Fortunately, Hades, who was the godboy of the Underworld, didn't join in the teasing. He'd had his own problems with bullies in the past, so was sympathetic to others who were picked on. But he did flicker a look between Epimetheus and her. Probably wondering why she was talking to a Titan.

Old prejudices die hard, she thought. Well, she was only doing a project with the Titans, not becoming BFFs with them. She was already friends with two of the most unpopular girls at MOA—Medusa and Pheme. She didn't need to buddy up with Titans, too. Because, as unfair as it was, nobody liked *them*!

"You know, your questions are starting to annoy me," Pandora informed Epimetheus frankly. Then she flounced off to sit at her usual table with Medusa and Pheme.

Medusa had already finished her lunch and was tossing some dried peas into the air to feed her snakes. She had a dozen of the reptiles growing from her head in place of hair. They were the result of a Snarkypoo invention of Athena's earlier that year. Snarkypoo had accidentally turned into Snakeypoo, a magical shampoo that had irreversibly changed Medusa's hair to snakes.

Surprisingly, Medusa seemed pretty happy with the way things had turned out. Those snakes adored her. They were like her pets, and she'd even given each of them names. And right now they were snapping those peas out of the air like it was the best game ever.

"Something wrong?" Pheme asked when Pandora set her tray on their table a little harder than usual.

Telling Pheme anything you didn't want others to know was a big mistake. That girl could spread gossip faster than a speeding chariot, and was proud of it.

But Pandora had no willpower when it came to Pheme. She sat down and spilled her guts. "That Epimetheus can be so annoying sometimes, don't you think?"

No doubt sensing a story, Pheme's eyes lit up. "Does this have to do with what happened in the hall before third period?" Her words puffed from her lips in little cloud-letters that formed above her head. They hung there, where anyone watching could read them.

When they didn't immediately fade, Pandora reached up to swat the letters away. "Are you talking about that box? The one the boys were playing Keep Away with that I, um, *accidentally* opened?"

"Yeah." Pheme licked her orange-glossed lips and leaned closer. "What was inside it?"

At that moment Pandora felt a bit sorry for Pheme. She recalled how crazy-curious she herself had been to know what was inside that fascinating box. But telling Pheme would be the same as telling the whole school. Talk about a blabbermouth! If you opened up a dictionary-scroll to the word "blabbermouth," you'd probably see her picture. Because that girl was the *definition* of the word.

Pandora took a bite of her ambrosia loaf. "Can't say," she said between bites. "Epimetheus asked me not to."

Pheme looked so disappointed that Pandora added quickly, "But I will tell you one thing about what was inside the box."

Pheme and Medusa both leaned forward now. Their eyes fastened eagerly on Pandora's face. Luckily, Medusa

was wearing her stoneglasses. They were like sunglasses, except they protected mortals (like Pandora) from being turned to stone by Medusa's gaze.

"It was *bor*-ring," Pandora informed them.

Medusa made a *tsk* sound. "Well, that was illuminating."

"Not!" said Pheme with a look of disgust.

Suddenly Pandora noticed yet another bubble aimlessly drifting along the high ceiling overhead. The green one. Those box bubbles sure were lasting a long time before popping.

She pointed her fork at it. "Do you guys see that?"

Medusa and Pheme followed her fork and looked up. Medusa's beady-eyed snakes did too.

Pheme's forehead wrinkled in confusion. "What, the ceiling?"

"You don't see that . . . that green . . ." In the nick of

time she stopped herself from mentioning what had been in the box.

"That green what?" Pheme prompted when Pandora didn't finish her sentence. She must still have been hoping for some scoop she could spread around MOA.

"Hmm? Oh, nothing," said Pandora. But it bothered her that they hadn't been able to see the bubble when it was so obviously there.

She looked around the cafeteria, trying to determine whether anyone else had spotted the bubble. Across the room at the popular goddessgirls' table, Artemis couldn't seem to stop admiring herself in her hand mirror. And Athena was staring off into space with a loopy grin on her face, instead of reading a textscroll as she usually did at lunch.

Seated opposite from them, Aphrodite and Persephone had their heads together, like they were whispering to each other. Maybe they were discussing the kooky behavior of the other two girls, Pandora decided.

Her gaze slid back to Athena and Artemis. Then a new thought struck her. Could the way they were acting have anything to do with the bubbles that had bumped them? No. That didn't make sense. How could a bubble change someone's behavior?

Glancing at the table where the two Titans sat, she caught Epimetheus staring at her. Again. Godsamighty! He should draw a picture of her. It would last longer.

On impulse she made a goofy face at him. Then she quickly turned back to face her friends.

Pheme, of course, had noticed Pandora looking at the brothers. "I wonder why Zeus let those two Titans come to MOA?" she said.

"Yeah, why invite trouble?" Medusa agreed.

Instead of nodding in agreement, Pandora took a

few more bites of her ambrosia loaf. For some reason she found herself wanting to stick up for the brothers. Or for Epimetheus at least.

Yes, he said some annoying things. But at least he'd shown some interest in her. More than Poseidon had so far, she thought ruefully.

And Epimetheus had said she was smart. Imagine that! She was just about to speak up in his defense, when the loudspeaker on the cafeteria wall crackled to life.

"ATTENTION, STUDENTS OF MOA!" Everyone jumped as Zeus's voice boomed out of the speaker. "Principal Zeus here, so listen up. All third-period classes will be pre-empted for the rest of this week. Instead everyone will participate in my latest great idea—a science fair!"

At this news there were lots of cheers. And a few groans.

"Choose a partner," Zeus went on. "You'll work in teams. Your third-period teachers will fill you in on the details tomorrow. Meanwhile, start thinking of a project that will blow the sandals off the famous judges I've invited."

This announcement was a hot topic for the rest of lunch. When Pandora went to the tray return with her trash before leaving for her next class, Aphrodite, Persephone, and Ares were already there.

"Hades and I are going to be partners," she overheard Persephone tell Aphrodite. "Our research question will be, 'Do pomegranate seeds grow faster on Mount Olympus, in the Underworld, or on Earth?'"

That wasn't a bad project idea, thought Pandora. Certainly it was something that was testable, though maybe not in one short week.

Aphrodite looked over at her crush, Ares, a twinkle in

her blue eyes. "I have an idea for a project we can do. Let's test the question, 'Do girls have faster reflexes than boys?'"

In a flash she reached out and jokingly knuckle-punched Ares on the arm to "test" his reflexes. Then, dodging him before he could react (looked like boys really *did* have slower reflexes!), she took off running. They both laughed merrily as he chased her around the cafeteria toward the exit.

Pandora could see it was all in fun. She was sure Ares could have caught Aphrodite if he'd wanted to. But then again, maybe not. After all, Aphrodite was fast. She'd proved that by winning the two-hundred-meter race in the first-ever Girls' Olympic Games!

While following behind Persephone to the exit door, Pandora spotted that green bubble she'd seen earlier floating overhead. Slowly it drifted lower, reaching the exit at the same time Persephone did.

From a few steps away Pandora watched the bubble bump against Persephone's arm. "Anger," a tiny voice whispered.

Pandora's eyes darted around the room, studying faces. No one showed signs of having spoken the whisper. Or of having heard it either. Or of having noticed the bubble. Not even Persephone herself.

Just to be sure Pandora caught up to Persephone and asked, "Did you hear that? And did you see that bubble—"

Persephone frowned at her. "Bug off."

"Huh?" Pandora was taken aback. Persephone was usually super nice. It was weird to hear her say something so mean.

Just then Aphrodite came running up to them, laughing. Trying to escape Ares, she accidentally knocked into Persephone, though not very hard.

"Watch where you're going!" Persephone yelled, elbowing her.

Aphrodite stopped short, her face stunned. In fact, everyone who'd been close enough to hear Persephone reacted with shock. And, no wonder. Normally she was the one trying to make sure everybody got along. She never got mad at anyone!

"What're you all staring at?" Persephone growled. After glaring around the room, she turned on her heel and stormed off in a huff.

Aphrodite looked at Ares. "Ye gods. What's gotten into her?" she asked in surprise.

Good question! thought Pandora. And she was beginning to think she might know the answer. Only, she didn't know how what she was thinking could possibly be possible!

5

Zeus Snooze

"I WONDER WHERE PRINCIPAL ZEUS IS?" PANDORA asked Athena the next morning. They'd been sitting in Science-ology class for ten minutes. The second lyrebell had already rung, and he still hadn't shown up.

Athena shrugged nonchalantly. "Dunno." She didn't even look up from the *Teen Scrollazine* she was paging through.

“So how was the party last night?” Pandora asked, trying to get Athena’s attention. They hadn’t had much time to talk in their dorm room yesterday evening. Athena had gone to a party and hadn’t returned till Pandora was already in bed. Which was odd, because Athena hardly ever went to parties. Usually her idea of a fun way to socialize was in a study group.

At the mention of the word “party,” Athena perked up. “Oh, my godness! It was *sooo* fun! Some of the godboys were dunking each other in the fountain.” She giggled.

Pandora arched an eyebrow. The Athena she knew would’ve called such antics *immature.* Or sophomoric. Or some other big word. “You sure were out late.”

“Oh, well, the party didn’t go all that late, but . . .” Athena looked a little embarrassed. “I got lost on my way back to the dorm afterward.”

“But wasn’t the party in the cupola at the top of the

school?" asked Pandora. The cupola was an open-air domed room that you climbed a spiral staircase to reach. Athena had been there dozens of times before.

"Yeah." Athena giggled again. "I think I caught bad-direction-itis or something."

Or maybe she'd caught bubble-itis, thought Pandora. Could the bubbles from that box yesterday morning really have something to do with how Athena was acting? The impossible idea was starting to seem more possible by the minute.

Before Pandora could ask anything more, Zeus arrived. She watched him come into the classroom and amble over to the teacher's desk, shuffling his feet.

Sometime since yesterday he'd replaced Muse Urania's regular chair with a golden, carved throne like the one in his office. Now he tumbled into it, propped his golden-sandaled feet on the desktop, and surveyed the class with tired-looking droopy eyes.

Zeus's wild red hair looked even wilder than usual this morning. He obviously hadn't combed it in a while. His tunic was all wrinkled too. And it was the same color as the one he'd worn the day before. Was it the same one? Hadn't he changed clothes since then? He looked like he'd just gotten out of bed!

"Major bedhead," she heard one of the godboys murmur, echoing her own thoughts.

Zeus yawned and scratched his chest. After sighing big he looked over at Athena. "Theeny, you're in charge today," he told her. "Wake me up when class is over."

With that he unrolled Muse Urania's lesson planscroll, laid it over his eyes, and leaned his head against the back of his throne. Within seconds he was snoring loud enough to wake the dead all the way down in the Underworld.

Everyone looked at everyone else in surprise. Then

they looked at Athena, wondering what to do.

Seeing their stares, Athena's eyes got huge. "Um, like, don't look at *me*," she said in a panicky voice. "You all know what to do, right?" She wiggled her fingers toward the scrollboard at the front of the room, where the six steps of the scientific method were still on display. Then she giggled nervously. "Do whatever it says there, okay?"

Normally when left without teacher supervision for a few minutes, students would begin tossing magic spitballs or passing notes. But no one quite dared misbehave with Zeus in the room. Even if he was snoozing.

So instead everyone paired up with their partners to discuss their projects. *Screech!* Heracles dragged his desk next to Athena's so they could work together.

Screech! Screech! Epimetheus and Prometheus dragged theirs over to Pandora's. Getting to her feet, she

turned her desk around so that the three of them could face each other in a triangle.

"So what should we do for our project?" she asked the Titans as soon as they sat down. She had to speak loudly to be heard over Zeus's snores, which were at least twice as loud as a classroom of screeching desks and shouting students. If he could sleep through his own snores, it was doubtful *anything* could wake him.

Really, though, it was unlike him to fall asleep here in class. Just as it was unlike Athena to act ditzy, Artemis to primp, and Persephone to lash out at others.

Hmm. Curiouser and curiouser. Had the bubbles actually somehow caused all this? Had they bumped Athena, Artemis, and Persephone and changed their personalities? And was it possible that sometime since yesterday Zeus had been bumped by a bubble too? A bubble that had managed to change him from an energetic Zeus to a *lazy* one?

Or had she just been bumped by an imagination bubble that was making her imagination run wild?

Pandora glanced at her partners. "Hey, how about if we do the project question, 'Why is Zeus acting so bizarro-lazy?'" she suggested, only half-joking.

Overhearing her, Poseidon hooked his thumb in Zeus's direction. "Cut the guy a break," he said. "He's usually a ball of energy. Maybe he's just tired today."

"Yeah," said Apollo. "You try being King of the Gods and Ruler of the Heavens plus principal of MOA, and see if it's not exhausting work."

They were probably right, Pandora decided in relief.

"C'mon. Let's get serious," Prometheus urged, snagging her attention again. The two Titans began discussing project ideas. Pandora put in a word now and then. But mainly she was eavesdropping on the conversation Athena and Heracles were having over on her right.

They were trying to decide on a project too.

"What do you want to research?" she heard Heracles ask Athena. He was practically shouting to be heard over Zeus's snores, so it wasn't hard to listen in.

She watched Athena flutter a careless hand in the air. "Oh, whatever you think," she told him.

"You mean you don't have any ideas? You want me to choose?" asked Heracles. He looked surprised.

"Well, you're such a *strong* guy. Your ideas are bound to be much more *powerful* than any I might have." Athena giggled.

Heracles looked like he didn't know whether to be flattered by this or concerned about the way she was acting. But then he seemed to shrug it off. "Okay. How about we go with the question, 'Which are the best kind of clubs to use to destroy different beasts?'"

"Perfect!" squealed Athena. She clapped her hands

together in admiration. Now Heracles looked truly shocked.

Pandora knew how he felt. No way Athena would want to study clubs and beast-destroying. At least not the normal Athena.

Heracles was a different story. Even now his big knobby club, which he'd actually used to slay all kinds of monsters and beasts, was slung over his shoulder. He carried it wherever he went, and the MOA boys liked to *ooh* and *ahh* over it.

Thunk! Pandora turned to see that a hunk of clay the size of her fist had landed in the center of her desk.

"Earth to Pandora," said Prometheus. He and Epimetheus each had a hunk of clay too, probably taken from the supply closet. They were both busily making something out of their hunks. Epimetheus's had four legs. A table, maybe?

"So what do you think of our plan?" Epimetheus asked her.

"Awesome, right?" added Prometheus.

Pandora had no idea what they were talking about, but she didn't say so. She poked a finger into her clay ball. "Um, could you go over the plan one more time?"

Prometheus looked at Epimetheus. "Told you she wasn't paying attention."

"We're each going to create a new character for the Hero-ology game board," Epimetheus told her.

Hero-ology was taught by Mr. Cyclops. For one of their projects, each student in his class was assigned a small hero statue that they moved around on a humongous game board in the center of the classroom. Under the students' supervision, the heroes worked toward different kinds of goals.

"Look at the hero *I'm* making," Prometheus enthused.

He held up the clay statue of a man with bulging muscles, who was clutching a big flat pan.

Pandora cocked her head curiously. "Why is he holding that pan?"

Prometheus frowned. "It's a shield, not a pan. I'm not finished yet." He started working on the shield, adding heraldry emblems.

"I'm making a heroic animal. A rescue dog," Epimetheus added. He showed her the four-legged thing she'd thought was a table at first. She could see now that it was starting to resemble a dog. While she watched, he cast a spell that made it magically trot across his desk. He smiled when she laughed.

When Pandora didn't begin work on her own hero right away, Prometheus asked, "What's wrong? Don't you like the idea?"

"It was actually your idea, you know," Epimetheus

told her. "Remember yesterday when you said you wanted to help mortals? You said we should give them something. So we're giving them heroes."

"But what about my idea to find out why Zeus is acting so lazy?" She leaned in so Athena wouldn't hear the next thing she planned to say. "He isn't the only one acting weird. Have you noticed how giggly and ditzy Athena is acting?" Immediately both boys turned to stare at Athena.

"Stop!" Pandora hissed. "Don't *stare* at her! I just wondered if you'd noticed?"

"All girls are giggly," said Prometheus. He said this as if it were an absolute fact he'd seen carved in the wall of a temple somewhere on Earth.

"That's not true," said Pandora. "And Athena's usually not at all giggly. She's usually super brainy."

"So if you giggle, you don't have brains?" Epimetheus asked.

Pandora straightened. The way he said it made her suspicions sound dumb. "Okay, then. We'll do the hero thing," she told them. "But isn't the first step in the scientific method to come up with a question? By making heroes, what question will we be trying to answer?"

"Our question is going to be, 'What effect will adding heroes to the game board have on Earth?'" explained Epimetheus. "And our hypothesis is that creating more heroes is a good idea because they'll be able to help more mortals."

"Or maybe they'll create more problems?" countered Pandora. "In Hero-ology we get graded on manipulation, disasters, quick saves, and on how well our heroes succeed. Which means our heroes are always trying to outdo each other. Which also means they're forever going on quests and starting wars on Earth."

The two boys stopped working on their heroes, suddenly unsure. "I told you we shouldn't have asked her to join our team," grumbled Prometheus.

Uh-oh, thought Pandora. If they kicked her off their team, she might wind up having to do a project all by herself. "Wait! Did I say it was a bad idea? I don't *think* so. It's pretty good, actually."

A new thought came to her, and she snapped her fingers. "I know! I'll make a girl hero. That'll be fun."

"Sounds like a plan," said Epimetheus.

Prometheus nodded.

They continued discussing their project as they worked on their statues. Pandora molded her clay hero-girl to have wild hair and a long cape that fluttered out behind her. She also gave her a big question mark on the front of her chiton.

"I'm going to name her Curie," she said. "For 'curious.'"

"Mine's Alpha Dog!" said Epimetheus, getting into

the spirit of fun. "Because he's number one when it comes to hero dogs!"

Prometheus looked hesitant. "I can't think of a name for my hero."

"He's made of clay. How about naming him Clay?" suggested Pandora. Which made both boys crack up.

Time flew by as they worked on their little heroes. They finished right before the lyrebell rang, and decided they'd take their statues to the game board the next day.

But then Pandora said, "Wait a sec. I just thought of something. The Hero-ology room will be empty during lunch, so why wait? We won't bother anyone if we take our heroes there now."

"Sure," said Epimetheus.

"Yeah, why not?" Prometheus agreed. So, after leaving the room with their little statues, they all headed down the hall to Hero-ology.

The classroom was empty when they got there. Like Pandora had figured, everyone had gone to lunch already. Even Mr. Cyclops. They slipped inside and went over to the game board in the center of the room.

The game covered the top of a table about the size of two Ping-Pong tables set side by side. Its three-dimensional world map showed colorful countries dotted with castles, villages, roads, and hills. The countries were surrounded by oceans filled with small sea monsters, mermaids, and scaly dragons that really moved!

Dozens of three-inch-tall hero statues already stood atop the board here and there. The Titans each chose a spot and set their heroes on the map.

But Pandora walked around the board, considering the various countries. "Let's see. Where should you go, little Curie?" she murmured to herself.

"What's this?" Epimetheus asked a few seconds later.

Pandora turned her head and saw him standing by some shelves against the classroom wall. He had picked up a wooden horse from a shelf to examine it.

The horse was about the size of a lunch box, plus legs, a head, and a tail. Naturally someone who liked animals the way he did would be interested in it.

"It's Athena's," Pandora told him. "A toy she brought from home. Usually she keeps it in our dorm room, but I guess she must be using it for something in class this week."

"So that's the famous Trojan horse?" said Prometheus. He went to stand by his brother, and they both gazed at it with interest.

"You've heard of it?" Pandora asked.

"Sure, everyone has. It's famous on Earth," said Epimetheus.

Earlier that year all the MOA students had been abuzz

about the horse too. Athena had used it to end the Trojan War! She'd tricked the team of classmates in charge of the Trojan heroes by offering the horse to them as a gift.

Little had they known that she'd filled its hollow stomach full of Olympic hero statues. Once the horse had been allowed inside the gates of the Trojan fortress, the Olympian heroes had jumped out and won the war.

Thinking of Athena made Pandora think of Athens, which had been named after that brainy girl. Staring back at the game board again, Pandora finally made a decision.

"Here you go," she told her hero. Then she placed her on the spot marking the city of Athens. By the time she turned to look at the boys again, they'd already put the horse back on its shelf.

"So what do we do next? For our project, I mean?" she asked. "We know mortals need stuff, but what exactly will our heroes do for them?" She stared off into space and tapped her chin with one finger, thinking. "Hmm. What do mortals need?"

"More pets," suggested Epimetheus. He didn't look like he was joking either.

"You would say that," said Prometheus, rolling his eyes in a teasing way. "Wait. I know. They need gold."

"Yeah. Or jewels," said Epimetheus.

Pandora cocked her head, considering. "Why would they need that?"

"To buy stuff," Epimetheus explained.

"Can't we take a shortcut? Just skip the gold and give them the stuff they really need so they don't have to buy it?" asked Pandora.

"But we don't know what they need," Prometheus protested. "Only *they* know what they need."

"Then why don't we go talk to them?" she suggested

as they headed out of the classroom. "Number two in the scientific method is research. Tomorrow during class let's go down to Earth and ask mortals what they need."

"You know? That actually makes sense," Prometheus agreed.

"Yeah, good idea," Epimetheus said, high-fiving her.

Pandora smiled as she reached up to slap hands with him. "I'm starting to like this plan!" she said. It would be nice to help other mortals, especially since she was a mortal herself.

And even better, this was turning out to be a good project. With a little luck on their side, maybe they'd even win the fair!

6
Titan Flight

THE NEXT DAY WHEN THE LYREBELL RANG FOR third period, Pandora met Epimetheus and Prometheus at the front office. It was jam-packed.

Pandora waved to get the attention of Zeus's administrative assistant. "Ms. Hydra? Can we get an Earth pass?"

Earth passes were like hall passes; only, they gave

students permission to travel to Earth during class time. Because of the Science-ology fair, lots of other students were in the office getting passes too. Like Pandora's group, they needed to do research on Earth for their projects.

Ms. Hydra looked super busy, trying to take care of everyone. Her nine heads were zooming back and forth on long, serpentine necks as they dealt with all the students clamoring for her attention.

Her green head, which was grumpy even on a good day, greeted Pandora and the Titans with a sour expression. "Hold your horses! I may have nine heads, but I only have two hands," it exclaimed. "I'll get to you in a minute." Too bad they hadn't gotten her sunny, smiling yellow head instead.

Several minutes later the three science partners finally had their pass and were pushing through MOA's big bronze front doors. On the way out Pandora reached for a pair of winged sandals.

"You'll need to put some on too," she told the Titans. "And you'll have to help me with mine. I'm mortal, so I can't make the wings work on my own."

"We can't use the sandals either," said Epimetheus, shaking his head. "They don't work for Titans, only Olympians."

"Oh," said Pandora, "I didn't know." She opened the bronze door and tossed the sandals back into the basket. Then she faced the brothers again, hands on her hips. "What are we going to do, then? We can't walk the whole way. It would take us forever to get to Earth and back."

"No worries. We have our own way of travel," said Prometheus.

"We call it Titan Flight," said Epimetheus. "C'mon." After the three of them took the granite steps down to

the courtyard, he spoke to Prometheus. "Fire up, Bro. Time's a-wasting."

Prometheus pulled an object about the size of a pickle from the pocket of his tunic. He tucked it into his fist, letting the top of it poke up about an inch. Then Epimetheus stacked his fist on top of Prometheus's fist, wrapping his fingers around the part of the object that was sticking out.

Together the two godboys murmured the same magical chant:

Basket for three
Come to me.

Then their fists jerked apart and they both let go of the object. In a flash it magically transformed into a large, square woven basket. The basket hovered in the air for a few seconds, then dropped to sit on the ground. The top of it was about even with Pandora's shoulder. And it did look big enough to hold three people.

Still she was a little disappointed. "A basket?" she asked. "That's what you use for Titan Flight?" She'd been hoping for something more unique and amazing.

"Just wait," Epimetheus said mysteriously.

Whoosh! She jumped back in surprise as an enormous balloon suddenly inflated from the basket's middle. Eight cords, each set about two feet apart, rose along the rim of the basket. Quickly the cords threaded themselves through holes in the bottom edge of the balloon, catching it before it could float away.

"A flying balloon? Awesome!" said Pandora, bouncing with delight. "How does it work?"

"It's powered by U-fire," said Prometheus.

"Huh?" she said.

"That stands for 'Underworld fire,'" Epimetheus explained. "Get in and you'll see."

He cupped his hands together so she could step into them. Then he gave her a boost over the side of the basket. After she'd hopped inside it, the two Titans hefted themselves in too.

In the middle of the basket's floor sat a small ceramic pot. She walked around it. Flames rose from it, but its fire didn't seem to have a fuel source.

Epimetheus noticed her confused look. "You know that thing we held when we were saying our chant?" She nodded. "It contains a single spark of U-fire," he told her. "The chant's magic ignites it. Then the fire heats the air, which fills the balloon to lift it."

"Did you get the U-fire from Hades?" she wondered aloud. That seemed hard to believe. Hades might not taunt them, but he didn't seem overly fond of them either.

Epimetheus shook his head. He and his brother had begun testing the cords that attached the basket to the balloon, making sure they were secure. "No. From our dad. Zeus banished him to the Underworld after the war."

"Since he couldn't be around to protect us anymore, he gave us the spark so we'd have the gift of flight," added Prometheus.

Their dad was in the Underworld? This was news to Pandora. She tugged on the cord nearest her, testing it like she'd seen Epimetheus and Prometheus do. Once they were satisfied that all was ready, Epimetheus called out:

Underworld fire,
Take us higher—
Earthward bound
Where mortals are found.

Pandora braced her feet and grabbed the side of the basket as it swiftly rose high in the air. And soon they were sailing away from MOA and downward from Mount Olympus, the tallest mountain in all of Greece.

For a while Pandora waved to other pairs of MOA students skimming the ground in winged sandals. But then she lost track of them as the balloon sailed faster and farther.

The breeze cooled her cheeks as they zoomed past puffy white clouds. Looking over the side of the basket, she could see their balloon's blue-gray shadow as it fell across the forests, grasses, and lakes below. Everything was so beautiful from up here. She almost hated for the ride to end.

All too soon, though, they began their descent. "Here we come, Earth!" Epimetheus yelled.

Below, Pandora saw an amphitheater, a round stone

temple, houses, roads, and a market called an agora. But the biggest landmark of all was the enormous limestone Temple of Zeus. It had six columns across the front and thirteen on each of its sides. And each column was nearly five times as tall as Zeus himself!

"Looks like we're in the city of Olympia," said Epimetheus.

"Where should we touch down?" Prometheus asked.

Pandora pointed below. "Maybe behind Zeus's temple?"

Epimetheus nodded and guided their balloon lower. It wasn't until they'd landed and stepped out of the basket that Pandora began to shiver. "Brr. Why is it so cold here?" she asked, wrapping her arms around herself.

"Good question," said Prometheus, who was shivering too.

"I've got goose bumps," added Epimetheus.

With chattering teeth the Titans recited a magical "undo" chant. It was basically their original chant, only they said it backward:

Me to come

Three for basket.

Instantly the balloon deflated and disappeared into the basket, which then shrank to pickle size again. Epimetheus pocketed it, and the trio walked around the side of the temple.

Prometheus had some coins, so they stopped at the nearby agora and bought three hooded cloaks to keep them warm. Soon they were standing in front of the temple.

Right away they saw a group of mortal youths

hurrying down its front steps and heading their way. Pandora peeked past them into the temple and gasped at the sight of the gigantic ivory and gold statue of Zeus himself. This temple was one of the most famous in all of Greece. And the statue of Zeus was one of the Seven Wonders of the ancient world!

"Hello? Excuse me," Pandora called to the youths. Hearing her, they paused. "Can I ask you a quick question?" Without waiting for their reply, she rushed on. "What do you need? I mean, what would you wish for if you could have anything?"

One bold youth didn't hesitate to answer. "A new coat!" he said.

A maiden passing by with only a thin shawl around her shoulders said, "Yes! A warm one!"

A gray-haired woman coming down the temple steps had also overheard. "Or how about a bright, hot fire

that never goes out?" She was wrapped in a half-dozen shawls, but still she shivered with cold. The whole group of mortals cheered her idea.

"Yes! We're freezing. And we can't even cook our food these days," said the maiden.

"Why don't you just build a fire?" asked Epimetheus.

"Bah! Try it yourself and see what happens," said the woman with all the shawls. "The fires on Earth have gone out and cannot be lit again. Even the fires in Zeus's temple."

Pandora peered back at the temple and saw it was true. "That's awful!" She sent the Titans a pleading glance. "What about the fire balloon? Why don't you—"

"Yeah, let's give them U-fire," Prometheus urged his brother.

Epimetheus put a hand over the pocket where he'd stashed the magic pickle device. Reluctantly he shook

his head. “You know we can’t. We swore an oath to Dad never to share it.”

“Oh, please!” the maiden begged. “If you have fire, we desperately need it!”

Prometheus hunched his shoulders and rammed his hands into his pockets. “I know we promised Dad. But still. It’s mean not to help.” He sounded frustrated at Epimetheus’s refusal.

“And you say I’m the one who acts before thinking?” chided Epimetheus. “U-fire could actually make things worse here. Dad told us it could prove as dangerous as that box of ours in the wrong hands.”

Just then a cold wind whipped up and blew back his hood.

“Look! His skin! It shimmers,” said the shawl-bundled woman. “Which Olympian gods are you?” she asked eagerly.

The boys didn't answer.

"Epimetheus and Prometheus aren't Olympians," Pandora told her. "They're T–"

"Titans! The sons of Iapetus," someone guessed before she finished. The crowd began to grumble.

"So that must be why we're cursed and can no longer make fire," an old man said. "Because Zeus has invited Titans to Mount Olympus!"

"Yes! It's Zeus's fault!" someone yelled.

"And the fault of these Titans!" someone else added.

"What? No. That isn't true," Pandora protested.

But no one was listening to her. And the crowd was getting angrier by the minute. Soon the mortals began to advance on the two Titans. And on Pandora, too! Apparently they also held her responsible simply because she was mixing with the Titans. It was guilt by association!

"Let's get out of here!" shouted Epimetheus.

7

Eew!

EPIMETHEUS TOOK PANDORA'S ARM AS HE AND Prometheus began backing away. With his other hand he pulled out the magic pickle device and brought forth the balloon basket.

The mortals' eyes widened in astonishment as the flames of Underworld fire whooshed up, inflating the balloon.

"Fire! They have fire, but they won't give us any!" someone yelled.

The two Titans jumped into the basket. They pulled Pandora inside after them, while reciting their flying chant all in a rush:

Underworldfire,
Takeushigher–
MountOlympusbound
Whereimmortalsarefound.

In the nick of time their basket lifted from the ground. *Whoosh!* They soared higher, gaining altitude. The three of them peered over the edge of the basket. Down below, the angry crowd still swarmed before the temple, shaking their fists.

Pandora took off her cloak and asked the boys for

theirs. Then she tossed all three cloaks down, hoping they'd at least help three mortals keep warm.

"I think this problem is bigger than our game board heroes can handle," said Epimetheus.

Pandora nodded. "We'd better tell Zeus, don't you think? When he finds out about this suffering, he'll know how to set things right."

The flight home seemed to take forever. But eventually they broke through the clouds, and the majestic Mount Olympus Academy—always an imposing sight—sprang into view. Built of polished white stone that gleamed in the sunlight, it stood five stories tall and was surrounded on all sides by dozens of Ionic columns. Low-relief friezes were sculpted below its peaked rooftop.

From overhead they glimpsed Principal Zeus and his wife, Hera, in the olive grove to one side of the courtyard.

Pandora scrambled out of the basket the minute they landed, and ran for the grove. Behind her she heard the balloon deflate. Then the Titans' footsteps were pounding closer to her as the boys followed.

When they got close enough, they could hear Zeus and Hera arguing. Or rather Hera was arguing. Zeus was smiling lazily up at the sky, appearing undisturbed by her ranting.

He was lying on a bench under an olive tree, sunbathing in his tunic. Unsure if it was wise to intrude, Pandora and the two Titans stopped at the edge of the grove to listen in.

"You said you would help me move some walls in my store *right away*," Hera railed. "But it's been two days, and you still haven't shown up to do it."

Zeus yawned. "I'll get to it, sugar pie."

"Don't you 'sugar pie' me," she said, folding her arms. She was probably the only person on all of Mount

Olympus or Earth who could get away with talking to Zeus like that.

"Oh, speaking of pies, would you mind getting me some lunch from the cafeteria, sugarplum?" Zeus asked.

"What? Get it yourself, you . . . you lazybones!" With that, Hera stormed off.

Once she was gone, Pandora and the two Titans burst into the grove.

"Principal Zeus?" Pandora began breathlessly. "There's trouble down on Earth? All the fires have gone out and need to be re-lit?" She knew she was making sentences into questions, but she was so upset, she couldn't help it.

"Later," said Zeus, yawning again.

"But mortals are cold and they can't cook," said Epimetheus.

"Whatever," said Zeus.

"Do you know what it's like to be without fire?" Prometheus demanded. He was getting really annoyed.

"You can't leave them that way," Epimetheus said. "They could freeze to death!"

"What do I have to do to catch forty winks around here?" Zeus whined. "I'm going someplace quiet." He stood and trudged away.

Stunned by his uncaring attitude, the three of them watched him go.

"Know what I think?" said Prometheus as they headed out of the grove a minute later. "I think the trouble on Earth is Principal Zeus's fault. I think he's gotten so lazy that he's neglecting the mortals there."

"You could be right," said Epimetheus. "Even the fires in his own temple were out, remember?"

It was true, but hearing the Titans criticize Zeus bothered Pandora.

Back in the courtyard Prometheus quickened his pace toward the front steps of the Academy.

"Where are you going?" Pandora called after him.

"To Hero-ology. I want to make some changes to my hero statue," Prometheus said over his shoulder. "So he'll be better equipped to help mortals deal with their lack of fire."

"What kind of changes?" Pandora asked, running to catch up with him. Epimetheus was right behind her.

"I'll give him weapons to hunt animals. That way, mortals will have fur coats," said Prometheus.

"No!" Epimetheus and Pandora exclaimed at the same time. They followed him through the front doors of MOA and then up the marble stairs.

"It's not the animals' fault that Zeus is lazy," said Epimetheus as they entered the Hero-ology room.

"Yeah, can't we figure something else out?" asked

Pandora. But Prometheus wouldn't listen.

When they reached the game board, Epimetheus tugged at his brother's arm to try to stop him. Prometheus shook him off. *Whap!* In their struggle they accidentally knocked a half-dozen little heroes into the Mediterranean Sea.

"Oh, no!" said Pandora as her girl hero statue splashed in.

Everything they did to their little statues on the game board actually happened to the corresponding real mortal heroes living on Earth. So that meant that the life-size, living, breathing heroes on Earth might be drowning! They could even get eaten. Because not only were the seas and oceans real, but the beasts that lurked in them were too.

"Hurry! We have to save them!" She stuck her hand into the sea, going elbow deep. The boys reached in too.

"Eew!" Pandora wailed as she fished around for her hero-girl. "I think a sea serpent just slobbered on my arm!"

Luckily, she was able to find Curie and scoop her out. The clay figure looked okay, if a little damp. Just as she and the Titans rescued the last of the six heroes who'd fallen into the sea, the classroom door flew open.

Mr. Cyclops, the Hero-ology teacher, came in. "What are you all doing in here? Get away from that board this instant!"

The three of them jumped back from the game board as if a bunch of sea monsters had leaped from the oceans and bitten their noses.

Mr. Cyclops put his hands on his hips. The single eye in the center of his forehead blinked at them. His only eyebrow scrunched up in irritation. "I asked you a question. *What* are you doing?"

"Working on our Science-ology project?" Pandora squeaked nervously.

"Which is?" asked Mr. Cyclops.

With the Titans' help Pandora quickly explained. Before they could finish their explanation, though, Mr. Cyclops was already shaking his head.

"This may be a game board but this *isn't* a game. You can't just add heroes to the board willy-nilly," he said. "Doing so could have serious consequences down on Earth." The single eye regarded them sternly for a few seconds. Then he said, "Please remove all of the new statues you've added."

"But–," said Pandora.

"Now," Mr. Cyclops commanded.

Pandora reluctantly wrapped up and pocketed her girl hero. The Titans scooped up their heroes too.

"Guess it's back to square one?" she murmured as they left the Hero-ology classroom.

"There is only one day left before the fair this Friday. We don't have time to start a whole new project," Prometheus grumbled. He and his brother both looked glum.

"Are you really going to wimp out?" Pandora asked them as they headed for the cafeteria. "Because I'm not. We know what mortals need now. We just have to think of a new way to help them get it. So put your thinking caps on."

"I think mine's broken," said Epimetheus, smiling slightly. Pandora gave his arm a playful punch. "Well, fix it." She wasn't giving up on the possibility of winning yet!

Just then they passed the stairs. Glancing up, Pandora noticed Athena standing on the landing, looking bewildered.

"Psst!" Athena waved her closer.

"You guys go on. I'll catch you later," Pandora told the boys. As the two of them continued on to the cafeteria, she took the stairs up.

"What's wrong?" she asked when she reached Athena.

"Well, you won't believe this, but I lost Woody," said Athena. "You know—my Trojan horse? The one I brought from my home in Triton down on Earth? I had him in our room. And then I remember taking him somewhere. But now I've totally forgotten what I did with him!"

"Don't worry," Pandora told her. "Woody's in the Hero-ology room. I saw him there a few minutes ago."

Athena snapped her fingers. "So that's where I left him! I can't believe I forgot. How bubble-brained is that?" Far from being upset, she burst out laughing at her own silliness.

Bubble-brained? It sure seemed that way! Watching

Athena head downstairs, Pandora got a mental picture of that blue bubble bumping Athena's forehead just two days ago. *Hmm. The bubbles. The Trojan horse. The bubbles. The Trojan horse.* Her brain seemed to be working on some kind of connection between the two.

Ye gods! she thought as an idea finally took shape.

Epimetheus and Prometheus had admitted they knew all about Athena's Trojan horse trick. What if their box of bubbles was actually a devious version of the same trick? A cunning Titan plot to get revenge on their dad's enemies—Principal Zeus and the Olympians at MOA!

Now that Pandora had gotten to know Epimetheus a little better, she didn't want to believe he could be capable of such a betrayal. Still, he was likely as loyal to the Titans as she was to the Olympians.

MOA was her home and she loved it. She'd even dyed

her golden hair with streaks of blue to match the school colors. All things considered, that was a pretty mild way to show loyalty. Maybe Epimetheus and Prometheus had gone to even greater lengths to show their loyalty to their fellow Titans!

Had Epimetheus been lying when he'd said he hadn't known there were bubbles in the box? He and his brother had been awfully interested in Athena's Trojan horse in the Hero-ology room. Maybe they had come to the Academy with their own trick horse.

Only, instead of a toy horse full of Olympian warriors, *their* Trojan horse was a box full of trouble bubbles!

8
Trouble Bubbles

PANDORA HUFFED AND PUFFED AS SHE RAN TO the cafeteria the next afternoon. Her last-period class, Gym-ology, had gotten out late, and she didn't want to miss dinner.

They'd started learning Beastie-ball last week. They'd studied the rules and practiced dribbling and throws. But today they'd had their first actual game.

When the ball had come her way, her teammates had yelled, "Feed the beast!" So she'd dribbled down the court, heading for the beast that had stood waiting at the end. Its mouth had been open wide, ready for her to toss the ball inside.

How many teeth did that beast have anyway? she'd suddenly wondered. *One . . . two . . .*

"Keep your focus," Coach had reminded her. So she'd stopped counting and kept on dribbling. Soon she'd been only ten feet from the goal. Things were going great.

But then she'd noticed that Antheia, who was on the opposing team, was wearing an awesome wreath in her hair. Its flowers were constantly changing colors. How had she gotten it to do that?

Whack! While Pandora's attention was on the wreath, someone had hit the ball away in the middle of her dribble. The other team had stolen the ball from her! *Oops!*

Her teammates had been annoyed with her for losing the ball. Could they blame her, though? She'd *tried* to follow the coach's advice. It was just that everywhere she looked there were so many fascinating things to pique her curiosity!

Now, as Pandora entered the cafeteria and got into the dinner line, her troubles bubbled back up inside her. Who could she talk to about her bubble box suspicions?

Principal Zeus? No. She didn't want him to know she'd caused all the trouble in the first place by opening a box that didn't belong to her. He might punish her.

Normally Athena was good at solving puzzles like this one. But since she'd been bubble-bumped, she wasn't her usual brainy self. Still, maybe if Pandora could talk some sense into her, they could puzzle things out together.

After grabbing a plate of nectaroni from the eight-

handed serving lady, Pandora glanced over at the popular table. Athena wasn't there. Neither were Aphrodite, Artemis, or Persephone.

Disappointed, Pandora continued on to her usual table. She arrived just in time to hear Medusa complaining to Pheme, "Hey, you got more nectaroni than I did. That lunch, er, dinner lady must like you better."

Sometimes Medusa was sensitive to imagined slights, so at first Pandora didn't think much of it. She set her tray down. "Want some of mine?" she offered.

Medusa brightened. "Yeah. Thanks."

Pandora stared in dismay as that snaky girl then scooped most of the nectaroni off Pandora's plate. She'd hardly left her anything to eat!

"Where were you at lunch today?" Medusa asked, handing back Pandora's nearly empty plate. "I didn't see you."

"With Epimetheus and Prometheus," said Pandora. "We were—"

"Why are you hanging around with them?" Medusa interrupted. "Do you like them better than me? I'm your friend too, you know. You should only hang out with me from now on, okay? Pinky swear?"

Pandora gaped at her. "Huh?" This was over-the-top behavior, even for Medusa. It was true that the two of them were friends. However, Medusa had never seemed to care about her all *that* much.

In fact, when they'd been roommates in third grade, Medusa had sort of driven Pandora away by answering her questions with more questions. Like if Pandora said, "Have you done your homework?" Medusa would answer, "Why do you ask?"

Or if Pandora said, "Do you think Poseidon's cute?" Medusa would answer, "Do *you* think he's cute?" Finally

Pandora hadn't been able to take it anymore and had requested a room reassignment.

"And you know what friends do?" Medusa went on before Pandora could reply. "They give stuff to their friends."

Medusa looked over at Pheme. "Like that cute bracelet you're wearing. Can I have it?"

Pheme put her hand under the table to hide the bracelet. "Nuh-uh. It's my favorite, and I want to keep it."

"Okay, be that way," Medusa said, pouting. "Some friend you are!"

Just then her attention was snared by something across the room. "Wow! I wonder where Iris got that adorable scrollbook with the rainbows on it. I've got to have it or I'll die. Just die! I'm going to go ask her to give it to me." She jumped up and ran after Iris.

Pheme and Pandora watched her go in surprise.

"Wow! That girl just put the *g* in 'greedy,'" said Pheme.

"Yeah, I agreedy. I mean, I agree," said Pandora. Medusa hadn't even eaten any of the nectaroni she'd taken from Pandora's plate. Maybe she hadn't asked for it because she was hungry, but because she wanted to *possess* it.

Had Medusa been bumped by a "Greedy" bubble since the last time Pandora had seen her?

Pandora looked over at the popular goddessgirls table again. Her heart sank when she saw that it was still empty. Where was Athena? The urge to talk over her troubles was overpowering.

She knew she shouldn't tell Pheme her suspicions. Still, the words were rising up in her throat, ready to spill. She opened her mouth.

Luckily, before Pandora could speak, Pheme stood up. Her eyes were pinned on Medusa. "I think I'll go find out what is up with her," she said. "It could be something that everyone else at MOA should know about." Eyes gleaming, she dashed off.

Pandora finished her dinner alone. Then she piled up her tray with Medusa's and Pheme's trays, and took all three to the return. After leaving the cafeteria, she rushed up to the girls' dormitory on the fourth floor.

She stopped by her room just long enough to check for Athena. But she wasn't there, either. If Aphrodite was in, maybe she'd know where Athena was. Pandora headed farther down the hall.

Then she had an even better idea. She would tell Aphrodite that Athena, Artemis, and Persephone—her three best friends—had been bubble-bumped. By now Aphrodite must have noticed how odd they were all acting. Working together, maybe they could hatch a plan to fix things.

If they could do that, they'd foil the Titan brothers'

plan—if they really did have one—to take revenge on the Olympians and overthrow Zeus.

She knocked on Aphrodite's door.

"I'd *love* it if you'd leave a message," said Aphrodite's voice.

"Can I come in?" Pandora eagerly called through the door.

No reply. She knocked again.

"I'd *love* it if you'd leave a message," Aphrodite's voice repeated.

Then Pandora noticed the heart-shaped wipe-off notescroll hanging on Aphrodite's door. She'd never seen it before, so it must be new. Attached to the note-scroll was a pink feather quill pen. The voice seemed to be coming from it.

"Are you a talking pen?" she asked. No reply. She tried knocking a third time.

"I'd *love* it if you'd leave a message," Aphrodite's voice said yet again.

The feather pen must be knock-activated, Pandora decided. Aphrodite obviously wasn't here. She could be anywhere on campus or even out shopping at the Immortal Marketplace. Quickly Pandora took the pen from its holder and began writing on the heart-shaped scroll.

Urgent! Can you come to my room? ~Pandora

She made the top of the *d* in her name into a question mark curl, like she always did.

Then, even though she had no idea how long it might be before Aphrodite got her message, she went to her and Athena's room to wait.

She'd been in too big of a hurry when she'd stopped by their room minutes before to notice something. Athena had redecorated her bulletin board. Gone were

the pictures of scientists that Athena normally adored. Instead she'd pinned up drawings of cute mortal heroes and godboys cut from various copies of *Teen Scrollazine.*

Pandora's eyes widened when she noticed a test-scroll on Athena's desk with a B minus grade. Normally Athena made straight A pluses. Something was absolutely, definitely up with her!

Pandora paced for a couple of minutes, hoping Aphrodite would hurry up and come. Then she picked up the glittery Magic Answer Ball that was on the shelf above her desk, and sat on her bed.

These melon-size balls were made by fortune-telling oracles and were sold in the Immortal Marketplace. They were supposed to offer solutions to problems, but hers had never worked quite right. It always made oddball suggestions that didn't quite make sense.

Still, she had nothing to lose by giving it yet another

try while she was waiting for Aphrodite. She held her hand out and set the ball in her palm.

"Magic Answer Ball, how can I stop those bubbles from making trouble?" she asked it. Then she tossed the ball into the air.

It hovered there for a few seconds, spinning crazily. Then, still suspended in midair, it stopped spinning. Solemnly it spoke its magic answer: "Hope."

Pandora gaped at it. "Hello? Hope? You think I should sit around and just *hope* things work out all right on their own? Well, you know what I think?" she told the ball as it silently sank to rest upon her open palm again. "I think you are *hope*lessly broken."

Just then Aphrodite knocked on her door, cracked it open, and poked her head in.

Pandora tossed the ball aside and jumped up. "Ye gods, am I glad to see you!"

"I just got back from Cheer practice. What's up?" asked Aphrodite.

"Bubble trouble," said Pandora. "Have you noticed how weird Athena is acting?"

Aphrodite shrugged and came inside. She was wearing her blue and gold uniform and had her pom-poms. "Sort of, I guess," she said. "She was late for Cheer and couldn't seem to remember the steps in the routines. But everyone has an off day."

"It's more than that. You know that Titan boy Epimetheus?" said Pandora. "Did you hear about what happened last Monday?"

"I heard you opened that mysterious box of his," said Aphrodite. "Pheme told me. And everyone else."

"Well, what you don't know—what nobody knows except the Titans and me—is that there were ten bubbles inside that box. All but one escaped when I opened it."

"Bubbles?" Aphrodite laughed. Then, seeing how serious Pandora looked, she stopped. "Really?"

"Yes, really," said Pandora.

"Well, that's definitely an odd thing to carry around in a box. But what does this have to do with Athena?"

"I saw one of the bubbles pop against her face," said Pandora. "And when it did, it whispered, 'Ditz.' Then another one bumped Artemis and whispered 'Vain.' And remember in the cafeteria when Persephone got so mad at you?"

Aphrodite nodded. "Yes. So?"

"Well, right before that happened I heard a bubble pop on her arm and whisper 'Anger.' Pandora paused. "Do you see what I'm getting at?"

Aphrodite tossed her pom-poms onto Athena's bed. "Let me get this straight. You actually think MOA has been invaded by personality-changing bubbles? That's a little hard to swallow."

"I have evidence." Pandora pointed at Athena's bulletin board. "Exhibit A: No more scientist pictures."

Aphrodite studied the board. "Maybe she's just in the mood to change things up a bit. Doesn't prove she's had a personality makeover."

Pandora got the test-scroll from Athena's desk and held it up so Aphrodite could see the grade on it. "Exhibit B minus," she announced.

Aphrodite's blue eyes rounded as she peered at the test-scroll. "Whoa! Athena made a B minus? That's impossible!" She certainly looked worried *now.*

Just then someone knocked on the door. "It's me, Artemis. I want to show you something. Can I come in?"

"Remember what I told you," Pandora whispered to Aphrodite. "About Artemis being bumped by the 'Vain' bubble." Then she called out, "It's open!"

When Artemis entered, both girls stared at her,

momentarily speechless. Then, at the same exact time, they sank to sit next to each other on the edge of Pandora's bed.

Because Artemis, who usually couldn't care less what she wore, was now dressed in a fabulous long purple chiton decorated with sparkly diamonds. A magnificent necklace strung with dozens of real gold beads and baubles was wrapped around her neck.

But that wasn't all. She was also holding a dog in her arms. Not one of her usual three big slobbery dogs, though. This one was new—a small white dog with bright eyes, a wagging tail, and a pink bow on its head.

"Like my outfit?" Artemis asked them, striking a pose in the doorway.

"Uh, sure," said Pandora, shooting Aphrodite a *See what I mean* look. "But who's that?" she asked, looking at the dog.

"Oh, this is Cutie Pie," Artemis explained. "She's my new magic accessory dog. I bought her at the Immortal Marketplace today. Watch this." Artemis touched a finger to the dog's bow. "Purple plaid," she commanded. The dog's glossy white fur instantly changed color and pattern, turning to purple plaid fur!

"What happened to your other dogs?" asked Pandora.

Artemis flicked a careless hand in the air. "Oh, they don't go with my outfit, so I left them in my room. But I think I might have to give them away."

"Give them away?" Aphrodite echoed in shock.

"Uh-huh. I mean, they're getting dog hair on my clothes and chewing on my sandals. It simply won't do." Artemis nuzzled the white dog, saying to it, "But you go with everything I wear, don't you, Cutie Snooty Patootie Pie! And since you're not real, you don't shed or make messes!"

Pandora leaned over and whispered to Aphrodite. "Exhibit C."

"Yeah, for *Cutie Pie*–crazed," Aphrodite whispered back.

Pandora nodded. "Or *costume*-crazed." Usually Artemis cared nothing for fashion. And she *loved* those three drooly dogs in her room! The normal Artemis would never, ever consider giving them away.

"What did you do with your bow and arrows?" Pandora asked suddenly. As goddess of the hunt, Artemis was an expert archer. An Olympic champion, in fact. She carried her bow and arrows everywhere. *Normally.*

"Oh, I'm thinking of giving up archery," said Artemis. "It just seems so . . . so unfashionable, you know?"

At that moment the door opened and Athena walked in still dressed in her Cheer outfit. A look of confusion came over her face as she glanced at the other three girls.

"Oops," she said, backing out of the room. "Guess I got the wrong door." She giggled. "Sorry to barge in on you, Aphrodite."

"Wait," said Pandora, jumping up to go after her. "This *is* your room, not Aphrodite's."

"It is?" Athena curled a lock of her long brown hair around a finger.

"Yes," Aphrodite and Pandora said at once. Artemis didn't say anything. She'd spotted Pandora's half-open closet and had gone over to study the clothing hanging inside it.

As Athena came back into the room, she stared blankly around it. A flicker of recognition finally entered her eyes when she focused on the new pictures on her bulletin board. "Oh, yeah," she said, giggling again. "Silly me."

Pandora looked from Athena to Artemis. Speaking

to them both, she said, "Can I tell you guys something for your own good? You are not yourselves right now."

"She's got a point," Aphrodite chimed in. "Artemis, you never cared about fashion before—"

"Are you kidding?" Artemis interrupted. She pulled out one of Pandora's chitons and held it up, checking herself out in the full-length mirror. "I *live* for fashion. Ask anyone."

Pandora turned to Athena. "As for you, no offense, but you're acting more featherbrained than brainy. Truth is, I think you and Artemis are both under some kind of spell."

Athena scrunched up her nose, looking confused. "Spell? Oh, I'm not very good at spelling. Not if a word's more than four letters long." She held out her hand, showing three fingers. Then she giggled once more and stared off into space.

Pandora tried again. She had to get through to them! "Athena, you're usually a whiz at math, remember? But now you can't count to four? I'm telling you—something *is* wrong with you."

Artemis, who was still admiring her reflection, overheard. She shot an alarmed glance in Athena's direction. "Does she have spots? A rash? I hope it's not catching." Worriedly she studied her reflection in the mirror again. "Red spots would *definitely* not go with my purple outfit!"

Tearing herself away from the mirror at last, she edged around Athena and headed for the open door. "I think I'd better go to my room. I can't risk marring my delicate complexion."

The second she left, Medusa's snaky head popped in. She scowled at Athena, Pandora, and Aphrodite. "How come you didn't invite me to your party? Are there any

snacks I can have?" She held out an enormous empty bowl, waiting pointedly.

"Exhibit, um," Pandora whispered to Aphrodite. She'd forgotten which letter her exhibits were up to. "Exhibit M for Medusa," she said at last. "I didn't see it happen, but I think she was bubble-bumped too. By a 'Greed' bubble."

"Did someone say 'party'?" Athena asked. She bounced on her toes, clapping. "Count me in. I *adore* parties."

"Sorry, no party," Aphrodite announced.

"Phooey," said Medusa. Whirling around, she and her empty bowl took off.

"Oh, ungood." With a look of disappointment Athena plopped down in her desk chair. She pulled her Spellology textscroll from the pile on her desk and began reading it upside down.

Ungood? Pandora could hardly believe her ears.

Had Athena really said that? It wasn't even a word.

"Godness, this is getting crazy," said Aphrodite.

"Believe me about the bubbles now?" Pandora asked her.

Aphrodite frowned. "I don't know what to believe. But something is definitely going on. One thing I don't get, though. Why hasn't anyone else seen the bubbles but you?" They were both speaking in low voices, so Athena wouldn't hear.

"Yeah, I haven't figured that one out myself yet," said Pandora.

"Well, we've got to get to the bottom of this." Aphrodite stood, picked up her pom-poms, and headed for the door.

Pandora stared after her. "Where are you going?"

"To find that box," Aphrodite told her. "And get some answers."

"Wait for me," said Pandora, going after her. Just then there was a small explosion, and the two girls turned in surprise.

"Oops!" said Athena. A curl of smoke rose from a pile of ashes at her feet. The residue of a botched spell. It was impossible to say what the ashes had been a minute ago.

"I'm not sure we should leave her here alone," Pandora murmured to Aphrodite from the side of her mouth. "She's a little too bubble-brained right now."

Aphrodite nodded, then said to Athena, "Come with us, okay? We're going to the boys' floor."

Athena leaped up and squealed in delight. "Woo-hoo! Let's get this party started."

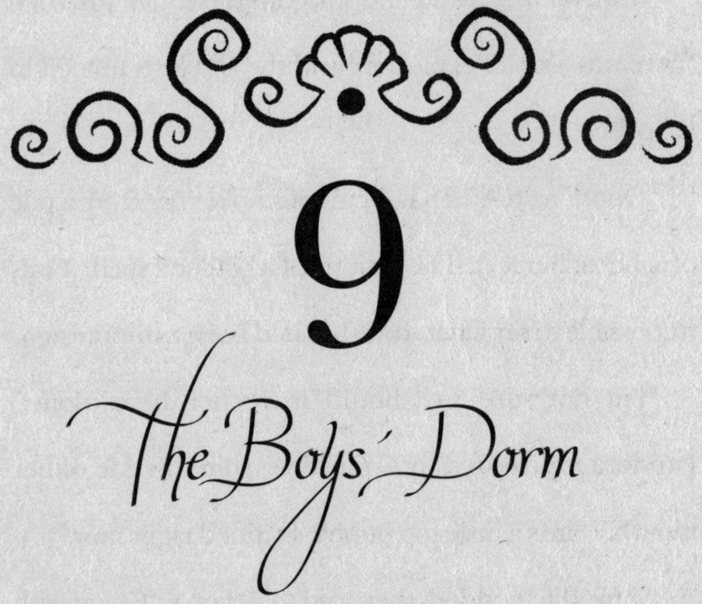

9

The Boys' Dorm

A MINUTE LATER PANDORA, ATHENA, AND Aphrodite were sneaking up to the boys' dorm on the fifth floor. Athena was still holding her slightly charred Spell-ology textscroll, and Aphrodite had her pom-poms.

As they took the stairs up, Pandora tried explaining to Athena that they weren't actually going to a party.

"Then what are we doing?" Athena asked blankly.

"Good question," said Pandora. She looked at Aphrodite. "Are we going to sneak into Epimetheus's and Prometheus's room? Steal the box? What are we going to do with it if we get it? What if they're in their room?"

"Then we'll confront them with our suspicions," Aphrodite said firmly.

"What if this was all a Titan plot to overthrow Zeus?" Pandora went on, giving voice to that fear for the first time. She was so keyed up that questions began spilling out of her one after another. "What if Epimetheus and Prometheus are under their dad's orders to blow us to smithereens if we get too curious? I don't even know where their room is. Do you?"

"It's at the end of the boys' hall," said Aphrodite. "I remember Ares mentioning it when those two Titans first came to MOA."

Aphrodite had only answered her last question,

Pandora noticed. Probably didn't have an answer for all her other ones. Pandora didn't either.

Athena giggled again. "This party sure is weird so far."

Rolling her eyes, Aphrodite opened the door to the boys' hall. "It's a surprise party, Athena," she said gently. "So you need to be very, very quiet."

"Okeydoke," whispered Athena. Pressing her thumb and forefinger together at the side of her mouth, she made a motion as if to zip her lips shut.

Pandora followed the other two girls through the door. Technically speaking, girls weren't allowed up here except for special events. She had gone to a party in the common room at the end of the boys' hall once. But she'd never really had a chance to look around.

So now, as the three girls tiptoed down the hall, she whipped her head back and forth, studying everything. Some of the boys had decorated their doors and left stuff in the hall. That made it easy to identify whose room was whose.

For instance, one door had a big poster-scroll tacked on it that showed Apollo and Dionysus playing in their band, Heavens Above. So that had to be their room. And leaning against the wall outside another door were several knobby clubs. Heracles' room, of course.

"Ares' room is down that way," whispered Aphrodite. "It's the one with the armor."

Sure enough, Pandora could see a life-size suit of armor standing next to one of the doors up ahead. As the girls drew near, it clanked into the middle of the hall. Then it held up a shield in one hand and a spear in the other to block their path.

"Halt! Who goes there?" it said in a metallic voice.

"Oh, bother. Not *you* again," Pandora heard Aphrodite mutter.

"Hello, gentle knight," said Athena, making a deep curtsy. "Remember us? We've come for the party."

Pandora's brows rose. *When had Athena and Aphrodite met the armor before?*

Seeing Pandora's curious expression, Aphrodite leaned over and whispered, "We sneaked up here a while back to find Heracles. Long story."

"Get thee hence from this hallway, fair ladies," the armor commanded. "This art the dorm of the godboys."

"Oh, please. Can't we go by just this once?" Aphrodite begged. She batted her eyelashes and gave the armor her best smile as she tried to sidle past. No go.

The armor held out his shield to block her. "No girl shall pass."

Studying the armor, curiosity rose in Pandora. "What's it like to be armor?" she asked the suit. "I mean, is it hard to lie down and take a nap, or what? And, hey,

are suits of armor friends with other suits of armor? Do they have families with little armor kids?"

The armor began swaying back and forth, as if uncertain how to respond to so many questions at once. Then its visor began to open and shut repeatedly. "Clankhead. Clankhead. Clankhead," it chanted over and over, waving its arms in crazy circles. It had gone totally haywire!

Athena giggled. "Aw, how cute. It's dancing!"

"Let's sneak by while it's confused," suggested Aphrodite.

Pandora nodded. "And before someone hears and comes out to investigate."

The three of them scooted past the armor and hurried down the hall. When they were directly across from the boys' bathroom, the door swung open. The girls skidded to a stop.

Out stepped Poseidon, clad only in the towel wrapped

around his waist. Besides that, he was wearing flippers and swim goggles and was holding his trident. Water dripped from his pale turquoise skin and puddled on the floor at his feet.

Seeing them, he squeaked in surprise. His eyes flicked from Athena to Aphrodite. "What are you doing here? Again. This floor is off-limits to girls, you know. I'm going to have to report you."

"If you do, we might have to mention to Pheme that you wear flippers and goggles in the bathtub," said Aphrodite. "Do we really want *that* news to get out?"

Poseidon's turquoise cheeks blushed pink. "Uh, no. You wouldn't really tell her, would you?"

"Not if you help us," Pandora put in quickly. "We're looking for the Titans. Which room is theirs?"

Poseidon pointed the pointy end of his trident off to the right. "Three doors down."

Aphrodite and Athena immediately headed off down the hall. But Pandora had noticed something curious. One of Poseidon's hands was hidden behind his back. What was he hiding? She leaned around him to see.

"Is that a tubby toy you've got there?" she asked in astonishment.

"No! It's um . . ." Turning even redder, Poseidon clutched the dolphin-shaped toy more tightly behind him. *Squeak!* went the toy. Looking mega-embarrassed, he whirled around and retreated back into the bathroom.

Pandora stared after him, not sure whether to laugh or what. Her crush played with tubby toys? And wore flippers in the bathtub? In that second her feelings for him changed a little.

Setting off down the hall again, she saw her companions heading for Epimetheus's room. And floating high

in the air a mere three feet behind Aphrodite was . . . *Oh, no!* Another bubble! The pink one. It was bobbing along in the air like it was plotting a sneak attack.

Forgetting to be quiet, Pandora shouted, "Aphrodite! Bubble! Run!"

"Bubble? Where?" Aphrodite said in alarm. Her golden hair swayed as she turned her head this way and that. She shook her pom-poms wildly, trying to bat away a bubble she couldn't see.

Then she ran. The wrong way, unfortunately. She turned back toward Pandora, and her nose smacked right into the pink bubble. *Pop!*

"Rude," a voice whispered.

Pandora recognized that voice. It was the same one she'd heard before, whispering "Ditz," "Vain," and "Anger."

Doors began to open along the hall. *Uh-oh!* The girls' loud voices had alerted the godboys to their presence.

Luckily, Epimetheus's door was the first to open. When his head poked out, Pandora shoved Athena and Aphrodite inside his room and barged in after them. Then she slammed the door behind her before the other boys could catch them out in the hall.

Epimetheus gaped at the three girls in disbelief. Prometheus stared too, from where he was working at his desk across the room.

"What are you—" Epimetheus started to say.

But Aphrodite interrupted him. "Oh, wow. Listen to this," she said, grinning in a goofy way. "I just thought of a song."

Dropping her pom-poms onto the floor, she tucked her right hand in her left armpit. Then she bent her left arm and began flapping it like a bird wing. *Boof! Boof-boof!*

Each time she flapped her arm, it squeezed her flat hand, producing horrible fartlike sounds. Sounds

that would normally have embarrassed the glamorous Aphrodite (or any self-respecting goddessgirl). But now she only laughed like it was the funniest thing ever. Everyone stared as she proceeded to armpit-play a tune, singing along with made-up words.

Godboy doodle went to town
Riding on a pony.
Stuck a feather in his cap
And called it nectaroni.

Athena giggled. "That is so, like, hilarious! Do another one!"

Aphrodite answered in burp-speak, burping between her words. "Be"—*burp*—"glad"—*burp*—"to"—*burp.* Then she obliged with another armpit tune, making up more words as she went along.

Now that Aphrodite had been bubble-bumped too, Pandora had lost her only ally. Concern for her friends welled up in her. She wasn't going to let these Titans get away with this!

She turned to Epimetheus. "See that?" she told him, pointing at her two friends. "Are you happy now?"

"No, we are *not* happy," Prometheus piped up. "Three girls just pushed their way into our room for no reason."

"Yeah, I thought girls weren't allowed on this floor," added Epimetheus, seeming a little offended by her attitude. "What's up?"

"I'm asking the questions here," said Pandora, frowning at him. "Where's that box of yours? The one I opened on Monday."

"None of your beeswax," Prometheus butted in.

"I know what you're up to," Pandora accused. She

glanced around the room, but didn't see the box.

The boys didn't have much stuff, she noted, probably because they hadn't been here long. However, the shelf by Epimetheus's desk had a whole herd of animal statues and a few scrollbooks about animals.

And there was also a picture of the twelve Titans who'd fought in the war against Zeus. Seeing it only heightened her fears that Epimetheus's allegiance was to the Titans. Who knew what these two brothers might be secretly plotting? Maybe even to start another war to dethrone Principal Zeus!

Pandora turned on him. "I thought you were nice. I actually liked you! But you came here to make trouble, didn't you? Are you plotting to hurt MOA."

Epimetheus looked startled. "Hurt MOA? We came here hoping to *stop* trouble, not start it."

"Oh, yeah?" Just then Pandora was distracted by the

sound of yet another *pop*. It had come from over by the window where Prometheus sat at his desk. By now she knew all too well what that sound meant.

"Thief," she heard the familiar bubble voice whisper.

10

Thief

PANDORA WHIPPED AROUND IN TIME TO SEE Prometheus go all shifty-eyed. His hand reached out, and he snatched Athena's Spell-ology textscroll from where she'd set it on his bed.

"Great. Number seven," Pandora groaned.

"What are you talking about?" asked Epimetheus.

Her eyes searched his face. It wasn't a guilty face.

Was it possible she'd been wrong to suspect the Titans? After all, Epimetheus wouldn't sic a bubble on his own brother, would he?

"Did you really not know there were trouble bubbles in that box of yours?" she asked.

"Trouble bubbles?" He looked genuinely puzzled. Then his expression changed. "Oh. Wait. You mean you were serious before when you said there were bubbles in that box?"

In that instant Pandora decided to take a chance on trusting him. What choice did she have? Because now they were the only two un-bubble-bumped people in the whole room!

"I was dead serious," she told him. Then words poured from her in a rush as she explained all that she suspected was going on.

Before she'd even finished, Epimetheus was shaking his

head doubtfully. "I was right there when you opened the box that day in the hall. I didn't see any bubbles fly out."

"Don't you get it?" Pandora spread her arms wide. "Nobody can see them but me. I wish I knew why, but I don't. So far I've seen four of them bump people—Athena, Artemis, Persephone, and Aphrodite. And I'm pretty sure two other bubbles bumped Medusa and Principal Zeus when I wasn't around. That's six. And the seventh one just bumped your brother. You didn't hear it whisper 'Thief'?"

"Nope," said Epimetheus, folding his arms. "And you know what I think? I think *you* have been bumped by a 'Crazy' bubble!"

"Oh, no!" Pandora pressed her fingers to her cheeks worriedly. "Really?"

Epimetheus rolled his eyes. "I was kidding. But where's the evidence that what you're saying is true?"

"There!" Pandora waved a hand toward her two friends. Aphrodite was still *boofing* armpit tunes, and Athena was helping her make up words.

Out of the corner of her eye, she saw Prometheus swipe something from Epimetheus's desk. She swung around and pointed an accusing finger at him. "And there."

"Who me? I didn't do anything," said Prometheus, trying to look innocent.

"Then show us what you're holding," challenged Pandora.

Epimetheus glanced over at his brother, who was standing by the window. He was facing them, with both hands behind his back. "Go on," said Epimetheus. "Show us what you're hiding, Bro. Just to prove her wrong."

"Fine," huffed Prometheus. "Here!" He tossed Aphrodite's pom-poms and Athena's Spell-ology textscroll onto the bed. "I was only borrowing the stuff."

But even as he spoke, he reached over and stole a little zebra statue that was on the shelf by Epimetheus's desk. He just couldn't seem to help himself from helping himself.

"Now do you believe me?" Pandora asked Epimetheus. "I really did hear a trouble bubble say 'Thief.' And now your brother is stealing stuff. And that"—she gestured toward her friends—"is not normal."

They both looked over at Athena, who had found a pair of scissors and was cutting paper dolls from her Spell-ology textscroll. Beside her Aphrodite was chewing the discarded bits of the papyrus scroll into spitwads, then thumping them to stick against the windowpane in the shape of a big heart.

"How obvious can it get?" Pandora asked Epimetheus.

"Well . . ." He looked a little less sure, but still not quite convinced that something was wrong.

Suddenly she remembered the mysterious words she'd noticed written on the box last Monday when she'd held it. Did they hold a clue that might help save her friends?

"Where is that box, anyway?" She started pacing the room, casually nosing around for any sign of it.

Instead of answering her, Epimetheus said, "Look, I think we should go talk to Zeus and see what he has to say about all of this." He started for the door.

Uh-oh! Pandora rushed ahead of him and plastered her back to the door. Epimetheus stopped short.

"Do you really think that's the best idea?" she asked him. "Like I said, he's one of the ones who got bubble-bumped. Remember how lazy he's been acting? That's so not him."

Truth was, she didn't want to admit her mistake in opening the box to Zeus. She'd rather get things fixed

back the way they were, before he found out about all this. Because he didn't have much patience with trouble-makers. And in this case, she was one!

"I think we should tell him anyway," said Epimetheus, trying to reach around her for the doorknob.

"Wait!" Pandora said desperately. She scooched over in front of the knob. "What if Zeus does the lazy thing and punishes you without listening to our story? What if he banishes you—and me—from MOA?"

"Banishes us?" Prometheus echoed. He looked at Epimetheus. "Where would we go? To the Underworld? To face Dad? He's not exactly happy with us right now."

Why not? Pandora wondered. She pressed her lips together hard, trying to stop the question from leaking out of her. Epimetheus looked so frustrated and unsure. She didn't want to make him feel worse by prying. It must be awful to have your own dad get really mad at

you. And it sounded like the brothers had no place else to call home!

"It's night already," she said gently. "Zeus could be asleep. Let's not wake him."

"We have to do *something*," said Epimetheus. "I don't know the extent of that box's powers, but I know it's mega-dangerous. Our uncle told us so when he gave it to us."

Pandora gulped at this reminder of danger. Epimetheus was right. They did need to do something, and fast. But involving Zeus should be their last option, in her opinion.

"There was some weird lettering on your box. What did it say?" she asked.

"I don't know," he told her. "We couldn't decipher it. Not even my uncle could."

"Maybe they're directions on how to defeat those bubbles. If I could see the box again, I might be able to

figure them out," Pandora hinted. "Well?" she said when he didn't make a move to get the box. "Can I see the box—*puh-leeze*?"

"We don't have it," Prometheus piped up. There was a string of Athena's paper dolls hanging from his pocket now. And Aphrodite's pom-poms had mysteriously found their way onto his desk.

Epimetheus nodded. "He's right. I left it in Zeus's office before Science-ology that day you opened it."

"Why?" asked Pandora.

"Because we thought it would be safe with him." He turned away and muttered something that sounded like, "But I guess we were too late."

"What did you say?" she asked.

Epimetheus looked over at his brother as if asking permission to reveal some secret. But when Prometheus shook his head, Epimetheus just shrugged and said, "Nothing."

Nothing, schmothing, thought Pandora. There was definitely something they weren't telling her.

"Well, Zeus probably stashed the box somewhere in his office like he does everything else he collects. I'm going to sneak in there and look for it," Pandora said decisively. Turning, she reached for the doorknob.

Athena had apparently been listening, because she said, "Sneaking into my dad's office is a great idea." Then her face scrunched up in confusion. "Or maybe not. I can't decide."

Pandora didn't want to imagine how much trouble she'd be in if she were caught. But if there was a chance that the box held the secret to returning everyone at MOA back to normal, she had to try.

"Okay. Let's go," Epimetheus said, taking a step toward her.

Pandora shook her head. "I'll go by myself. There's

no reason for the rest of you to risk getting in trouble too. Especially since I'm the one who opened the box and let the bubbles escape in the first place."

"No way. I'm coming," said Epimetheus. "Your search will go faster with help."

"Me too," said Prometheus. "I bet there are some awesome collectibles in Zeus's office." He rubbed his palms together in anticipation.

"What about me?" asked Athena.

"We'll need lookouts," Epimetheus told her. "Maybe you and Aphrodite could wait outside the office and signal if you see anyone coming."

"Yay!" said Athena. She jumped to her feet, clapping like she'd just won a prize.

Aphrodite, who had abandoned her spitballs, was busy working on a new armpit song. "What"—*burp*—"ever," she said carelessly.

"Okay, but don't blame me if we get caught," Pandora warned them. She was going to feel really bad if that happened, though. However, Epimetheus was right that the search of Zeus's office would go faster with help.

She opened the door a crack and peeked out of the room. There were still boys in the hall. She looked back at Athena. "Where's your Spell-ology textscroll?"

"Um." Athena looked around blankly.

Epimetheus frowned at Prometheus and held his hand out toward him, palm up. "Hand it over, Bro. And the other stuff."

With a sheepish expression Prometheus handed over the pom-poms, paper dolls, a couple of small animal statues, and what was left of Athena's cut-up Spell-ology textscroll. He'd somehow managed to steal it again.

Fortunately, the section of the scroll with the "hiding spell" was still intact. With a little help from Aphrodite and Epimetheus, Athena was able to cast the spell. It made all five of them invisible.

"Hurry. We can't be sure how long the spell will last," Epimetheus said as they silently left the room.

Pandora, Athena, and Aphrodite held hands as they sneaked along, so they wouldn't get separated. Halfway down the hall they passed Ares and Poseidon. Ares was busy trying to get his armor to work right. Wearing a robe now, Poseidon stood next to him, watching him work.

"What is wrong with you?" Ares asked the suit of armor. He bent its arms to its sides and held them there. But the second he let go, the arms whipped up again. "C-c-clankhead!" the suit stuttered.

Aphrodite stuck her tongue out and blew a raspberry at the armor as they went past. Athena giggled.

"Did you hear that?" asked Poseidon. He dropped to a crouch, glancing around wildly.

But Ares was so busy concentrating on his armor, he wasn't paying attention to anything else. He shook his head. "I didn't hear anything. Why are you so jumpy?"

"I'm not," Poseidon insisted. He still looked nervous, though. His face had paled and he clutched his trident tighter. What a scaredy-cat!

Pandora rushed the two goddessgirls onward to the stairs before they could make any more mischief. Good thing too, because the invisibility spell wore off the minute they all ducked out the door.

She doubted Ares or Poseidon would've really ratted them out even if they'd seen them. But there had been other boys in the hall as well. If they'd spotted the sneaking group, word would get around. Eventually Pheme would get wind of the news, and then Zeus would find out.

"I don't get what you see in that Poseidon," Epimetheus

said to Pandora as they started downstairs. "What a dippy guy."

Pandora shrugged. "He's the godboy of the *sea.* Of course he's going to be drippy. What do you expect?"

She was only pretending to think he'd said "drippy." Because she didn't want to tell him that she halfway agreed with him. In fact, she was beginning to wonder exactly what she saw in Poseidon herself.

Could it be that she was so used to worshiping him that she couldn't admit he was unworthy of her admiration? She'd think about it more when she had time. But right now they had other more pressing matters to deal with.

Like rounding up a bunch of dangerous bubbles!

11 Sneaking Around

THROUGH THE WINDOWS ALONG THE STAIRS, Pandora could see it was pitch black outside except for a scattering of twinkling stars. Fortunately, torches were set here and there in holders that angled out from the walls along all the school's stairs and hallways.

Prometheus seemed fascinated by these night-lights and asked about them. Pandora explained that

Hephaestus–the godboy of blacksmithing and metalworking–lit them each night from the fire burning in his forge.

When the five students reached the main floor, they moved soundlessly through the empty halls toward Zeus's office.

After a minute Athena whispered, "Sneaking around the halls this late is, like, so . . ." She seemed at a loss to describe it.

"Sneaky?" Pandora supplied. "Creepy? Spooky?"

"Yeah, all of those," said Athena.

"We're here," Epimetheus said when they eventually reached the door that led from the hallway into the school office.

"Athena, you and Aphrodite keep a lookout, okay?" Pandora reminded them. "And don't let each other out of your sight. Promise?"

Athena nodded, giggling for no reason at all. Aphrodite slouched against the wall and pulled a piece of gum from her pocket. After popping it into her mouth, she began smacking it loudly. "Yeah. Uh-huh. Whatever."

Pandora rolled her eyes, trying very hard to remember that Aphrodite couldn't help being rude at the moment. Putting her hand on the doorknob, Pandora turned it and pushed. *Creak!* The door swung inward. Epimetheus and Prometheus crept past her into the outer office.

She was reluctant to leave Aphrodite and Athena out here without supervision, but they really did need lookouts. Glancing back at them again, she asked, "What signal will you use to let us know if someone's coming?"

Right then Aphrodite let out a loud burp followed by two short ones that echoed down the hall.

"One long, two shorts. Got it," Epimetheus called softly back to them.

Pandora was unsure whether Aphrodite had actually meant that as a signal, or whether she'd just burped for fun. Either way, Pandora was looking forward to having the polite Aphrodite back. And the brainy Athena too.

She crossed her fingers that they'd find the box. And that the words on it would provide a solution to make things normal again!

Moving quietly, she followed the Titans into the office. As they passed the tall semicircular counter behind which Ms. Hydra usually worked, she saw Prometheus's hand reach out.

Quick as a whip, he snagged the small golden bell that sat on the countertop. Students rang it to get Ms. Hydra's attention if none of her heads were within earshot. The bell gave a startled little tinkle as he stuffed it into the pocket of his tunic.

“Put that back!” Pandora whispered. Caught red-handed, Prometheus hunched his shoulders. Then he grudgingly returned the bell to the countertop.

“Whoa! What happened here?” Epimetheus said. He spoke in a hushed voice even though there was no one else around.

He’d stopped outside Zeus’s office. Its door was hanging at an odd angle, swaying crazily by the top hinge. The two lower hinges were broken.

The creepiness of sneaking around in the middle of the night made Pandora speak softly too. “Oh, that. It’s no big deal. Happens all the time,” she told him. “Principal Zeus doesn’t know his own strength, so sometimes he swings his door too hard. Ms. Hydra will probably call a custodian to fix it tomorrow.”

The Titans managed to shift the door aside so they all could slip past. *Creak!*

Pandora tiptoed inside. Zeus's office was mostly dark. But luckily a bit of pale light filtered in from the stars and the full moon, which were visible through the office windows.

Clunk! "Ow!" Epimetheus grunted up ahead.

"You okay?" Pandora asked.

"Uh-huh," he muttered. "No thanks to Principal Zeus's housekeeping. This place is a mess."

"Eew, gross!" Pandora wailed softly as her sandal squished something. It had felt gooey and slippery like a banana peel. She stumbled over a couple of board games, then crunched what she guessed was one of the game pieces underfoot.

"It's always messy in here," she whispered to her companions as they searched for the box. "I'm pretty sure it's only like this because a trouble bubble is making Zeus lazy."

Epimetheus's voice floated back to her from somewhere by the windows. "You stick up for people. I like that about you," he said.

Pandora considered that as she bent and felt the tops of the chair cushions in front of Zeus's enormous desk. "And here I thought you thought I was annoying," she teased.

"Huh? No way," said Epimetheus. Then she heard him tell his brother, "Put that down." There was a dull *thunk* as Prometheus dropped whatever it was that he'd just tried to steal.

"I can't see a thing!" Prometheus grumbled. "I'm going to go get a torch. Be right back."

Pandora heard his footsteps cross the room. Once his brother was gone, Epimetheus spoke in a low voice. "There's something I need to tell you even though Prometheus doesn't want me to," he said. "It's about a prophecy. One that an oracle told my uncle. One that concerns you, I think."

"Me?" Pandora asked. Prophecies were exciting, amazing things. She could hardly wait to hear more.

"Our uncle warned Prometheus and me not to tell anyone because it would cause suspicion about the box. But that oracle? She predicted that one day a curious girl would open the box and bring forth trouble."

"Oh. Um, I'm guessing the trouble-bringing girl turned out to be me?" said Pandora, a little dismayed.

"Bingo. But don't feel bad. Prophecies have a way of coming true even if you try to stop them."

"Yeah," Pandora replied. It was weird to think that an oracle had known what she would do before she'd even done it, though. She never thought she'd be part of a prophecy!

"So anyway, that's why I avoided you when I first got to MOA," Epimetheus went on.

"You did?"

"You didn't notice?"

She shook her head, forgetting that he couldn't see her. She'd thought the Titans were avoiding everyone.

"My Uncle Epimetheus said that you were the most curious girl at the Academy," he told her.

"He knew me? Hey, wait a minute," said Pandora, as she suddenly put two and two together. "Did your uncle substitute teach a class at MOA one semester a few years ago?"

"Yep. He said you unleashed some weather disasters from a box in a storage closet, right?" Epimetheus asked.

Pandora blushed, remembering. "Oh, yeah. I sort of tried to forget about that."

"So anyway, I just wanted you to know that even though we avoided you, it was nothing personal. I mean, I like that you're curious, you know?"

Now that she thought about it, they had sat as far away from her as they could in Science-ology class. And their table in the cafeteria was far away too.

She heard him moving stuff around somewhere across the room, and realized she'd been just standing there thinking. She started searching for the box again. "So do you think that's why the box opened for me when it wouldn't for anyone else? And why I'm the only one who can see the bubbles?"

"Probably," Epimetheus said. "I'm sorry," he added. "Since I knew about the prophecy, I should've believed you about the bubbles when you first told me. I guess I just didn't *want* to believe what was happening. Everything seemed okay at first. And by then we'd given Zeus the box to protect, so—"

Oomph! "Ow!" Stumbling in the dark, Pandora pitched forward onto all fours. She wound up kneeling

in a square patch of moonlight that illuminated the floor in front of her.

"Are you okay?" Epimetheus asked, his voice full of concern.

"Um-hm. Yeah, I just tripped," she told him. "Over some empty bottles of Zeus Juice."

When she pushed up, Pandora brushed her long hair from her face. And found herself looking right at a pair of huge golden sandals. Sandals with feet in them. They were under Principal Zeus's desk. Which probably meant . . .

She went up on her knees and peeked over the edge of the desk toward the throne behind it. A tiny squeak left her, and she clapped a hand over her mouth to keep from shrieking in surprise.

Zeus! He'd been here the whole time, snoozing away in his throne! Couldn't he at least have snored like usual to let them know he was here?

"Pegasus?" Zeus mumbled sleepily. "Did you fetch my thunderbolts?"

His big hand reached across the desk and patted the top of her head. He'd mistaken her for his winged horse! Sparks shot from his palm. Luckily they went sideways. Otherwise her hair might've caught on fire.

"Good boy," Zeus said, obviously still half-asleep. Then he folded his arms on the desk, laid his head on them, and began to snore.

"What's going on?" Epimetheus whispered in alarm from across the room. "Is Zeus *here*?"

"Shh! Yes," she whispered back. "He's asleep at his desk." Keeping an eye on Zeus to be sure he didn't wake up, she began backing away on her knees. Then she froze in her tracks. Because she'd just noticed something.

In the crook of one arm, Zeus was cuddling a stuffed

horse that was a perfect likeness of Pegasus. And clasped in his other arm was—the bubble box!

RIINNG! RIINNG! Just then the fire alarm lyrebell went off!

Pandora's eyes bugged out. Zeus's blue eyes popped open. For a second they both stared at each other across the desk in silent astonishment.

Then she leaped to her feet. "There's a fire somewhere in the building. We need to get outside!"

Suddenly Epimetheus was beside her. Zeus blinked at them in confusion. "What are you two doing in here? What's going on!" he bellowed. Then he yawned. His eyes drooped shut, and his head sank onto his desk again.

Outside in the courtyard Pandora could hear the MOA herald shouting, "*Fire! Fire!* This is not—I repeat, not—a drill. Everyone file into the courtyard in an orderly fashion without further ado."

"Principal Zeus, wake up! There's a fire!" Pandora yelled. She and Epimetheus ran around the desk and each grabbed one of Zeus's arms, shaking him. Or trying to. He didn't budge.

"C'mon!" Epimetheus urged him.

"I think I hear your wife calling you," Pandora fibbed, figuring that might wake him.

Immediately a burst of energy surged through Zeus. He jumped to his feet. "Hera? Sugarplum?" he called, looking around. The mention of Hera sure seemed to bring back the old Zeus. But not for long.

When he didn't see her, his eyes closed again and his shoulders slumped forward. At least he was standing now, though. Pushing him from behind, they managed to get him to shuffle out of the office. Out in the hall, students were scurrying toward MOA's enormous bronze front doors and the courtyard beyond.

"Where's Prometheus?" Epimetheus called.

"I see Athena and Aphrodite up ahead," Pandora called back. "I'm guessing he's with them?"

Swept up in the crowd, she couldn't see over the heads around her and quickly lost track of Zeus, her friends, and Epimetheus, too. Soon she was out in the courtyard with everyone else. Most of the students looked sleepy, like they'd just jumped out of bed.

Artemis was wearing a lavish froufrou nightgown and long robe. She was holding her Cutie Pie dog in one hand and her hand mirror in the other. In the meantime, her three big dogs were excitedly bounding around among the other students. All dozen of Medusa's snakes were curled tightly to her head, still dozing despite the commotion. Next to her, Ares sported pj's bearing the logo of a sword-making company in the Immortal Marketplace called Mighty Fighty.

Spotting Hades nearby, Pandora went over to him. "What's happening? Where's the fire?" she asked.

"There!" Hades pointed up at a window in the school. Smoke was billowing from the Hero-ology classroom!

Zeus and the other teachers were gazing up at it. Zeus seemed to be having trouble taking charge of the situation. Instead of shouting his orders, he mumbled them, sighing and yawning.

Luckily, MOA's fire hoses still recognized his voice and obeyed him. Three of them magically rose from the courtyard fountain like long snakes. Thanks to the pumping system, which Poseidon had designed, the fire was quickly extinguished.

Pandora thought it was amazing that Zeus had managed to issue orders at all while under a Lazy spell. That kind of determination, power, and energy could only come from a true King of the Gods!

The students were told to wait outside while Zeus and some of the teachers went inside to investigate. On their way in, Poseidon suddenly ran out of the bronze doors past them, shrieking like his pants were on fire. Which they weren't.

"Fire! Save me! Help! Run for your lives!" he yelled. When he reached the bottom of the granite steps, he leaped into Hades' arms.

Hades staggered back under his weight. "Whoa! Get a grip, godboy," he said, setting Poseidon on his feet. "You look fine to me. And anyway, the fire's already been put out." Since Hades spent a lot of time in the Underworld with its molten rivers of lava, fire didn't faze him.

Some of the kids were grinning and trying not to laugh at Poseidon's antics. Medusa was blinking at him in surprise. Pandora knew that the snaky girl had once

had a crush on him too. But all that had ended around the time Principal Zeus had married Hera.

"I want my mommy," she heard Poseidon whimper.

Suddenly suspicious, Pandora peered at him more closely. Poseidon had his faults, but he wasn't a total wimp! To test out her suspicions, she pointed to the ground behind him.

"Hey, Poseidon, isn't that your shadow?" she asked. It was a ridiculous thing to say. But he fell for it.

"Eek!" At the sight of his shadow slanting across the moonlit marble tiles, he jumped a foot high. Then he dashed off to hide behind Apollo.

"What's up with him?" Epimetheus asked, coming to stand beside her.

"I think maybe the eighth bubble found him," Pandora said. "Maybe earlier tonight. Remember how he was acting in the hallway?"

Epimetheus grinned. "You mean dippy, er, drippy?"

For some reason she wanted to laugh, but she managed to stop herself. "No!" she told him sternly. "I mean—"

"Eek!" the turquoise godboy shrieked again. "Get away! Stop following me, you . . . you shadow!"

Epimetheus chuckled as Poseidon began running around. "Must've been a 'Chicken' bubble that got him. Or a 'Scaredy-cat' one."

Pandora felt a smile curve her lips, and this time she couldn't control herself. She giggled. "Well, he can't help it," she said, trying to stop. "Nobody acts normal when those bubbles attack."

"Show's over. Everybody back to bed!" the herald called out. Zeus had leaned from the Hero-ology window to signal that all was safe.

As everyone began filing back inside, Pandora wound up next to Poseidon. That's when she realized he

was wearing footie pajamas! Her eyes traveled from his feet to his face.

"I was worried something might nibble my toes while I was sleeping," he said defensively.

"Do you really think that's a realistic possibility?" she asked kindly as they pushed through MOA's front doors and went inside.

Before Poseidon could answer, Principal Zeus came down the marble stairs toward them. He had Prometheus by the scruff of his neck. "Pandora! Epimetheus! Get over here on the double!"

Uh-oh! thought Pandora. Though he'd yawned between each word he'd spoken, Zeus still looked and sounded thundering mad.

She and Epimetheus scrambled to obey. They reached Zeus just as he released Prometheus. Then the principal stood there and eyed all three of them, his arms folded.

"IT SEEMS THAT SOMEONE PURPOSELY SET THE HERO-OLOGY ROOM ON FIRE," he boomed in an accusing voice that echoed through the halls.

"What?" asked Pandora. "Who would do something like that?"

"You tell me," said Zeus. He opened his palm and showed them a charred clay statue holding a stick. Pandora sent Prometheus a sidelong glance. It was the hero statue he'd made for their Science-ology project. But why was it holding a stick?

"Mr. Cyclops has told me he found the three of you loitering around the game board earlier today. And you know what that makes you?" The three students shook their heads. "My prime suspects," Zeus informed them.

Then he looked at Prometheus. "You in particular. What were you doing in the hall outside the Hero-ology room just now?"

Prometheus shoved his hands into the pockets of his tunic. "All right. I admit it! I started the fire!"

Pandora and Epimetheus gasped. Other students were still filing around them, going back to their rooms. They overheard of course and started grumbling. She could totally understand them being mad. A Titan had almost burned down the Academy!

"But it was an accident," Prometheus went on. "I stole—I mean *borrowed* one of Hephaestus's night-light torches and used it to light that torch my hero is carrying."

So that's what the stick in the charred statue's hand was, Pandora realized. A tiny torch.

"I gave fire to my hero so he could use it to help other mortals on Earth," Prometheus explained. He glared at Zeus. "Because someone who *should* have been keeping the fires burning on Earth was too *lazy* to do it."

At this, Zeus made a strangled noise in his throat. He looked like he was in the mood to zap someone or even hurl a thunderbolt!

Godness, thought Pandora. *Prometheus better watch his words or he might end up as charred as his hero statue!* Although, now that she looked at the statue, it was actually more sooty than burned. Since mortals were suffering, he'd done a heroic thing, all right. But talking to the principal like this was a very bad idea.

Zeus pointed in the general direction of the Hero-ology room. "Everything that happens on that game board happens on Earth!" he roared. "Which means mortals have had a fire."

"Good! They were freezing," Prometheus said. "They need fire!"

"But not *wild* fire!" thundered Zeus, spreading his arms wide. "Fortunately, it's out now, so there'll be little

damage on Earth. Still, you must be punished for your rash action."

Then he wilted a little. "Only, I'm too tired right now to think up a fitting punishment." He shut both of his sleepy eyes. Then he opened them to slits to stare at Prometheus. "Therefore, you will decide your own punishment."

"I have an idea!" Epimetheus interrupted. "You could punish him with a spell to make him stop stealing. You know, like he stole that torch."

It was a crafty suggestion. But Zeus—even a lazy Zeus—couldn't be tricked so easily. He squinted at Prometheus, his blue eyes seeming almost to burn into the boy's mind.

"Aha!" Zeus said at last. He slowly rubbed his palms together, and sparks flew. The three students jumped back to avoid being struck by them. "I have looked into your mind, Titan. And I see liver."

"Liver?" Prometheus echoed.

"Yes," Zeus went on. "I have learned that you *hate* liver. Therefore, as your punishment, I proclaim that you shall dine upon it forevermore. As in—through eternity. Got it?"

Prometheus turned a sickly green. "No! Please. Anything but that!"

"Wait! This is partly my fault," Pandora protested. It wasn't fair that all the blame should fall on Prometheus. "Because of that box. I—"

"Enough! There's no excuse for what this boy has done." Zeus went to the front door, opened it, and whistled. From somewhere in the nearby forest came a loud *caw* and the flap of wings. On a mighty whoosh of air, an eagle flew from the treetops. It zoomed inside the Academy, circled them, and then landed on Zeus's shoulder.

He and the eagle both pinned Prometheus with their gazes. "In case you are tempted to disobey, this eagle-eyed eagle will be watching to ensure that you eat every bite of liver set before you from now on."

Immediately following this pronouncement Zeus yawned loudly. "I need a nap," he said as the eagle hopped from his shoulder to Prometheus's. All three students stared at it, and it stared back at them as Zeus turned on his heel and headed for his office.

What were they going to do now? Pandora wondered. That eagle would probably be keeping an eye on Epimetheus and her as well as Prometheus. And meanwhile Zeus still had the box.

12

One Last Hope

THE NEXT MORNING PANDORA WOKE TO THE sound of hammers and the scraping of furniture. It seemed to be coming from down below in the courtyard.

"What's all that noise?" Athena grumbled. She put a pillow over her head.

"Today's the Science-ology fair, remember?" Pandora told her. She hopped out of bed and ran to the window.

Down in the courtyard students were beginning to set up their displays. There were rows of tables, some with awnings overhead. Unusual gadgets and illustrated poster-scrolls already sat on some of the tables.

Athena's rolled-up poster-scroll was on her desk here in their room, just waiting to be displayed outside on the table she'd share with Heracles.

A sick feeling came into Pandora's stomach. Her team had nothing to display. She was going to fail the project. As were her partners.

Taking a deep breath, she pushed the thought aside. Because she had more important things than a mere grade to worry about. She dug around in her closet and came up with a butterfly net. She whipped it back and forth in the air a couple of times, making swishing sounds.

"What's that for?" Athena asked, peeking an eye out from under her pillow.

"Bubble hunting," said Pandora. "Near as I can tell, there's still one bubble loose in the school. If I can save one last student from being bubble-bumped, that'll be something, right?"

"Definid–definditpy–definity– Um, yeah," agreed Athena.

Quickly Pandora shucked her pj's and pulled a blue and gold chiton over her head.

Athena sat up and slid her feet into slippers that were beside her bed. Then she stared down at her feet in confusion. "These feel weird."

Pandora looked over at her and sighed. "Because they're on the wrong feet."

Athena giggled, then bent to switch left with right.

"See you in the courtyard," Pandora called as she made for the door.

"'Kay," Athena replied.

After taking the marble stairs down, Pandora stopped by the cafeteria to grab some cheese styx from the snack table. She didn't have time for a real breakfast. She was on a mission!

First thing she saw in the cafeteria was Prometheus, seated and staring at a plate piled high with liver on the table before him. He was kind of hard to miss because that eagle from last night was perched on the back of his chair.

It was peering over his shoulder, watching closely to be sure Zeus's orders were carried out. Prometheus was eyeing the pile of liver, his lips curled in distaste.

"OMG," she murmured to herself. "He looks sickly green, and he hasn't even taken a bite yet?"

"Oh, but he has," said Epimetheus. She hadn't noticed that he'd come up beside her. "That's a special plate he's eating from. Every time he takes a bite of liver, more liver

magically appears. He has to sit there and keep eating it until the eagle decides he's had enough. Breakfast. Lunch. And dinner. Forevermore."

Just thinking about that made Pandora turn a little green herself. She despised liver with a purple passion too.

"I'm sorry?" Pandora told him. She hadn't meant it as a question, but she was so upset that of course it came out that way.

"Yeah, well, that doesn't really help him." Epimetheus left her side and went to sit by his brother. With a heavy heart Pandora trudged outside to the courtyard.

She'd started across it, when Persephone walked by with her crush, Hades. "Will you shut up?" she was saying to him. She was obviously still under the spell of the "Anger" bubble.

Hades got steaming mad. "Fine. I will!" He turned on his heel and stomped off.

Watching him go, Persephone looked like she was going to cry. "I don't get it. Why am I acting like this?" she murmured under her breath.

"Because you were bubble-bumped," Pandora whispered, but not loud enough for Persephone to hear. The girl wouldn't understand anyway, and Pandora didn't have time to explain.

Keeping a sharp eye out for the stray ninth bubble, she wound her way through the science fair displays. Artemis was already at her table, holding her new Cutie Pie dog. She had partnered with Pheme for some unknown reason. Both girls were wearing heavy eye makeup. The title of their display was:

QUESTION: WHICH EYE SHADOW COLOR MAKES US LOOK THE MOST BEAUTIFUL?

Pandora was sure this choice of project had been Artemis's idea, but at least Pheme seemed to be enjoying herself too. Due to some kink in their experiment, the shadow colors on their eyelids were changing at a dizzying speed, randomly flashing new colors every few seconds.

It was a weirdly cool project, but Pandora had a hard time seeing the scientific merit in it. Next she walked past Medusa. She was in the middle of an argument with Iris and Antheia, who had the table beside hers.

"Oh, come on. You don't need all that room," Medusa told them. Then she proceeded to slide her poster partly onto their table, taking half of the other girls' space.

"Why are you doing this?" asked Iris, sounding annoyed.

"Yeah, you've got plenty of room on your own table," Antheia added.

In reply Medusa eyed them and pointed a finger

at the title of her project poster. The question she was apparently researching was: GIVE ME MORE.

It wasn't really a question at all, but who was going to argue about that? No one, that's who. Certainly not Pandora. Not with a snarky snaky-haired girl who also had the power to turn mortals like her to stone.

Pandora sent her an encouraging thumbs-up, and Medusa grinned at her. Then she called out, "Hey, can I have that butterfly net?"

Pandora sped up and pretended not to hear. *Now, where did that pesky ninth bubble get to?* she wondered, scanning the sky.

"What's wrong with you?" she heard Apollo say as she was walking along. He wasn't talking to her, though. When she looked his way, she noticed Poseidon was hiding under the table that he and Apollo shared.

Seeing her, Apollo pointed at Poseidon. "I don't know

what's gotten into this guy. He insisted on changing our project and redoing our poster at the last minute. It's embarrassing!"

Apollo gestured at their poster-scroll, which appeared to have been erased and hastily rewritten. It now read:

QUESTION: WHAT SHOULD YOU BE SCARED OF?

HYPOTHESIS: EVERYTHING.

Suddenly Apollo's gaze shifted to the granite steps that led up to the school. His expression changed to one of dislike. "Firebugs," he muttered.

Wondering what he was talking about, Pandora glanced over. She was just in time to see Epimetheus and Prometheus push through the front doors of the Academy. Prometheus was still looking a little green from all that liver.

As they descended the steps and began to walk through the fair, everyone shot them angry glances. "I knew we were right not to trust you," Kydoimos hissed at them as they passed.

It wasn't fair! Prometheus had only stolen fire because of that "Thief" bubble. Well, also because he wanted to help mortals. His heart was in the right place. So was Epimetheus's. But no one else at MOA knew that.

There had to be a way to fix things so everyone stopped blaming the boys. And so her friends didn't stay permanently weird. Capturing that ninth bubble might be the first step. So where was it?

Just then a light coming from above flickered in Pandora's eyes. She looked up at the sky and saw Hermes' chariot winging toward the fair. There were three passengers with him. Probably the science fair judges.

But there was also something else glinting in the sunlight overhead. Something closer. Something round and small and turquoise that was bobbing along in the air. She put up a hand to shield her eyes and saw . . . the ninth bubble!

Her heart started thumping. She had to pop it before it could strike yet another victim! As it moved beyond the awnings, she ran along the aisle trying to follow it. It streaked through the science fair, leading her on a not-so-merry chase.

"Come back here, you stupid bubble!" she called out as she zoomed after it.

In her haste she couldn't help knocking into people as she ran. Since they couldn't see the bubble and didn't know how important her mission was, they were understandably annoyed.

"Troublemaker," someone grumbled at her.

"You have no idea!" she yelled back. Because she *was* a troublemaker. When she'd released those bubbles, she'd caused *tons* of trouble.

Finally, when she judged she was close enough to the bubble, she jumped and swung. *Swish!* She whipped her net through the air, trying to capture the bubble.

Whoosh! Hermes' chariot zoomed down from the sky, sending a puff of air her way. The bubble did a few corkscrews in the air and dodged her net. Then it whipped away and headed for the chariot, which had just landed.

Hermes hopped out and opened its side door so his three passengers could get out. Pandora watched in dismay as the turquoise bubble zipped over and bumped one of them. *Pythagoras.* She recognized him from the pictures Athena used to have of him before she changed her bulletin board.

Pandora wasn't close enough to hear what the bubble whispered to him. She went closer. The minute the three scientists stepped from the chariot, she leaned over to the bubble-bumped one. "Pythagoras?" she asked.

He looked straight at her and replied, "No. I'm Aristotle."

"What?" Pandora knew that wasn't true.

"No, you aren't," another scientist said to him in surprise. "I am."

Ignoring him, Pythagoras made his way down the first row of student exhibits. He stopped at Kydoimos and Makhai's table and studied their project. It was all about mathematical shapes. The boys smiled at him, but their faces fell when he shook his head.

"I'm sorry," Pythagoras told them. "Your drawings are incorrect."

He pointed at their poster. "That's not a right triangle," he went on. "It's a *wrong* triangle. In any right

triangle there are four sides. The longest side is called the hippopotamoose."

Huh? There were *three* sides to a triangle, thought Pandora. And the long side of a right triangle was called the hypotenuse. Pythagoras should know that. He had even written a theorem about right triangles that had made him famous!

She trailed him as he continued on through the exhibits. "Geometry is the study of weather," he told one student. "Math is the study of fruit," he told another.

He must've been bumped by a "Lying" bubble! And the ridiculous lies he was telling left everyone flustered or scratching their heads in confusion. Still, because he was a famous scientist, no one dared contradict him.

Suddenly Pandora heard Athena squeal in that ditzy new voice she'd been using since she'd gotten bubble-bumped. At the same time Heracles yelled out, "Hey! That liver-bellied Titan is stealing my project!"

Pandora caught a glimpse of Prometheus, who was indeed trying to make off with Heracles' prize club from his and Athena's display. Which was impossible, since that club weighed a ton. Prometheus looked like he was making his getaway in slow motion as he dragged the club an inch at a time down the aisle.

Apollo and Ares quickly ran over to help Heracles confront Prometheus. *Godzooks!* thought Pandora. It was clear that a fight was brewing.

Just then she heard a buzzing sound. Snores. They were coming from the olive grove, right off the courtyard. Nobody snored that loudly except Principal Zeus.

Pandora raced into the grove. Sure enough, she found him there slumbering on a bench. The bubble box was in his lap, and his stuffed Pegasus pillow was under his

head. Had he wandered outside again after the fire and slept here all night?

"Principal Zeus!" she yelled. She had to get him to wake up long enough to help calm everyone down. But he didn't twitch a muscle. She called his name several more times but got no response. Just more snores.

Her eyes lingered on the box. His arm was covering the writing. If she woke him, would he let her examine it? Maybe not. He'd been pretty mad at her and the Titans last night.

For a split second she almost wished Prometheus were here so he could steal it for her. But, no, that wasn't fair. According to Epimetheus, the oracle's prophecy had foretold that she—a curious girl—would one day release the bubbles. And that had come true.

The oracle hadn't said, but maybe it was also up to her to figure out how to get things back to normal

again. Maybe she was the only one who could!

Slowly she reached for the box. Her fingers shook. What punishment would Zeus deliver if he caught her? Would it be liver for every meal, like Prometheus's punishment? Yuck!

Zeus snuffled and then turned on his side. *Thunk!* The box fell to the grass.

Eureka! Pandora snatched it up and studied the strange letters carved into the lid. Were they clues to help her foil those dastardly trouble bubbles?

Just like it had last Monday, the writing began to reshape before her eyes, forming words. Only, now she had enough time to actually decipher them: *Ditz, Vain, Anger, Lazy . . .*

Ye gods! It was only a list of the troubles that had been inside the box. That was no help at all! How she wished she'd never even *seen* this box! But what was done was done, she thought as she stood next to the snoring Zeus.

Just then he let out a loud snort. Pandora jumped, and her fingertip accidentally brushed the lock. It clicked open right away. Again she wondered why only she had the power to unlock this mysterious box. Because of the prophecy?

So now what?

She rested a hand on top of the box, trying to get a feeling for what she should do. For some reason she really wanted to open it. But maybe it was only her curiosity making her feel that way. Did she dare open it again? Would that make things better? Or worse? The questions whirled in her head.

Then a voice came from inside the box. Softly it whispered to her. "Hope."

This voice sounded a little different from the others.

A little more helpful. Or more like *hopeful.* Was it the voice of the last bubble?

Out of the blue Pandora remembered what the Magic Answer Ball had said when she'd asked it for help yesterday. "Hope," it had said. Had it been right after all? Would a "Hope" bubble truly be the answer to her problems?

"Okay, bubble," she warned. "Don't make me sorry I'm doing this."

Slowly she eased open the lid. Just like last Monday, she heard the rumble of thunder as she did so. Lightning flashed in the grove.

Zeus didn't bat an eyelash. But over in the courtyard students stopped arguing. A startled hush fell.

"I hope, hope, hope . . . ," Pandora chanted, unsure even then what she expected to happen.

Suddenly the box flew all the way open on its own.

There it was! The last bubble. Number ten. It glowed with a dazzling golden-yellow light.

It floated out, wafting upward. Uncertain, she reached up with her net, then thought better of it and lowered it again. Somehow she knew she should let this bubble escape.

As if in thanks for her trust, it swooped down and gently bumped her cheek. Softly, so that it didn't pop. "Hope," it whispered.

And just like that Pandora suddenly felt a little better. A little more hopeful that everything might soon be set right.

After gently bumping Zeus's cheek too, the "Hope" bubble whooshed off. Pandora raced after it, watching it float around the fair bumping everyone it passed. Each time it bumped into someone, it whispered, "Hope."

Immediately a smile would come over the bumped person's face. Then they would say something kind and hopeful to whoever was standing closest to them.

Pandora was right beside Athena when the "Hope" bubble bumped her forehead. There was a kind of reverse-popping sound–*Gloop*! Then the blue "Ditz" bubble reappeared. It had unpopped!

Surprised, Pandora dropped her net. Thinking fast, she then opened the box and held it out toward the bubble. There was the brief sound of thunder. Lighting flashed for a couple of seconds. Then—

Snap! She shut the lid and recaptured the blue "Ditz" bubble! "One down," she murmured gleefully.

Athena blinked a few times, then began to look like her old self. "Godness!" she remarked to Pandora. "I feel like my brain has been on vacation."

"Don't worry. It's okay now." called Pandora. Grabbing

her net again, she dashed off to follow the "Hope" bubble as it moved on.

She passed Epimetheus and Prometheus. *Bump! Gloop!* The red "Thief" bubble unpopped from Prometheus. It rushed upward, trying to escape.

"Help me!" Pandora called to Epimetheus. Tossing him the box, she leaped high and swung her net overhead, capturing the red bubble. "Gotcha, bubble!"

"Open it!" she yelled at Epimetheus, who had caught the box.

Seeing that the clasp was undone, he realized at once what was going on. And as soon as Pandora deposited the red bubble inside, he slammed the box closed on her command.

"That's two bubbles down," Pandora said happily.

"Sorry, Bro," Prometheus said. "I, um, think this is yours." He reached into his pocket and held out a small

skunk statue he must've stolen from Epimetheus's shelf.

Epimetheus took it just as the "Hope" bubble bumped him too. His face brightened. "Thanks," he said. "Don't feel bad about taking it, though. You were under a spell."

"C'mon!" Pandora told Epimetheus. She scurried off again with her net, and he followed. "Catch up with you later," he called back to his brother.

"I hope you know what you're doing," Epimetheus said as he jogged alongside her.

She grinned at his choice of words. "Yeah, me too."

Together they chased the golden "Hope" bubble through the fair. Since he couldn't see it, Epimetheus followed Pandora's lead. Whenever it bumped someone who'd been previously bumped by a trouble bubble—*Gloop!*—the trouble bubble would unpop and appear before her eyes.

Each time, Pandora was there to whip her net

through the air and scoop up the bubble. And Epimetheus would open the box. Thunder would boom and lightning would flash, but only briefly. Just long enough for her to tuck the trouble bubble into the box without letting any of the captured ones escape. Then Epimetheus would snap the box shut again.

Of course, to him her net and the box looked empty. But he understood what she was doing.

Bump! Gloop! "Sorry if I've been cross lately," Persephone told Hades.

Bump! Gloop! "I feel like I've been making misstatements," Pythagoras said to the students he'd been addressing. "Please excuse me if I have."

Bump! Gloop! "Ick," said Artemis, staring into the hand mirror she was holding. "I hope this isn't shadow on my eyelids. I'm going to wash it off and go get my dogs. See you," she told Pheme.

One by one, the "Hope" bubble brought comfort to everyone at the fair. And more important, it de-troubled all the bubble-bumped people.

All of them except Zeus, curiously enough.

13

Why, Why, Why!

"WHY IS MY DAD SLEEPING OUT HERE?" ATHENA asked. She, Pandora, Persephone, and Aphrodite had gathered around Zeus where he still slept on the bench in the olive grove.

"Because one of the trouble bubbles bumped him," Pandora told her. "The 'Lazy' one, remember?" The three goddessgirls sent her confused looks.

Pandora shifted the bubble box she held from one hand to the other. Epimetheus had left it with her while he'd gone to find his brother just now. "You don't remember?" she asked the others in amazement. She hadn't counted on this.

It took nearly ten minutes for her to explain to the girls that they'd all been bumped by trouble bubbles. "And the effects only went away after the tenth bubble, the 'Hope' one, made the other bubbles reappear," she informed them.

Pandora held out the box in one hand and patted its lid with her other hand. It was making those same weird noises she'd heard coming from it that first day. The other girls eyed it warily.

"The bubbles are in here now. Epimetheus and I captured them," she assured them. "All except the 'Lazy' one. And the 'Hope' one—it flew off somewhere." She

figured it was probably bringing hope to those in need wherever it went now—at least she *hoped* so.

"Well, that's quite a story," said Persephone when Pandora had finished.

"But it doesn't explain why my dad is still affected," said Athena.

"Maybe the 'Hope' bubble didn't bump him," said Aphrodite.

"It did, though," said Pandora. "I saw it happen."

"Then why didn't the 'Lazy' bubble *gloop* out of him?" asked Persephone.

"Maybe it was *afraid* to come out," suggested Athena. "Because it realized he's King of the Gods and he could zap it into oblivion if he gets mad enough about what it did to him."

It was an interesting theory, thought Pandora. But that didn't necessarily mean it was correct. Suddenly

another, much simpler theory occurred to her. "Or maybe the 'Lazy' bubble didn't reappear because it's *lazy*?"

Athena looked at her in surprise. "I never thought of that! Good thinking. I bet you're right."

Pandora smiled. Coming from the brainiest goddess-girl at MOA, this was high praise indeed. "It's only a theory," she said humbly.

"Is there a way we can test it?" Persephone wondered.

The girls stood there a minute, mulling ideas. Which wasn't easy with the bubble box making those weird noises the whole time.

"I know!" Pandora said at last. "Maybe we can trick the 'Lazy' bubble into believing its effect on Zeus has worn off? You know, get him to act all energetic for just long enough to make that bubble give up on him and unpop."

"Worth a try," said Athena. They all looked at Zeus, who was still snoozing.

Everyone jumped a little when Athena suddenly yelled, "Dad! Wake up!"

At the sound of her voice, Zeus opened one sleepy eye. "Huh? Give me one good reason to."

"Because today's the science fair," she said.

"Are the judges here?" Zeus asked, yawning.

Athena nodded.

"Good. Then you don't need me." Closing his eye again, he rolled over onto his side so his back was to the girls.

"But Principal Zeus," Persephone tried. "Won't Pegasus be waiting for you to feed him?"

"He's fine," Zeus mumbled over his shoulder. "I told Mr. Cyclops to feed him."

"I bet you have a bunch of appointments to take care

of today," said Aphrodite. "Hadn't you better return to your office?"

"Ms. Hydra can handle things," Zeus said with another yawn. "Now I command you to leave me alone." Within seconds he was snoring again.

Athena frowned. "What're we going to do? Nothing seems to trouble him enough to make him get up."

She was right, thought Pandora. Only the threat of big trouble—like the fire in the Hero-ology classroom—was likely to overcome Zeus's laziness. But starting a new fire was out of the question. Then she thought of something that might be equally effective.

"Uh-oh, Principal Zeu-uus," she singsonged. "I think I see Hera coming this way, and boy, does she look mad. Did you ever knock down that wall in her store she asked you about?"

That did it. Zeus sat bolt upright. "Wha—? Sugar pie?

Here? Mad?" he said, looking around wildly. His hair was sticking up in all directions, almost like he'd been struck by one of his own thunderbolts.

Fully awake—at least for the moment—he leaped to his feet. "Listen," he whispered. "Don't tell her you saw me!" Then he took off running toward the back exit of the grove as fast as he could.

Pandora was after him just as fast. It wasn't long before the "Lazy" bubble reappeared on its own. *Gloop!*

"Got you!" she yelled as she caught it in her net. She stuffed it back into the box. *Snap!*

Instantly Zeus stopped in his tracks. He wheeled around. All traces of his former laziness were gone now. Vanished as soon as the "Lazy" bubble was nabbed and returned to the box. She couldn't believe it. Her plan had worked!

Only, now Zeus stood before her, powerfully tall,

energetic, and *angry*. His eyes went to the box. "What are you doing with that?" he demanded.

"Um, here, you can have it," Pandora told him, handing the box over.

Zeus took it, examining it closely. "I thought I heard the lid snap shut a minute ago. But how could that be? I created this box myself and locked it forever years ago. No one can open it. No one except me."

So that's why the box thundered and flashed lightning every time it opened, Pandora realized. Because it had been created by Principal Zeus, Ruler of the Heavens!

Zeus's piercing blue eyes surveyed Pandora and the other three girls who'd gathered around him. "Explain."

"I opened it," Pandora admitted shakily. "The box, I mean."

"WHAT?" Zeus roared. "HOW?"

Suddenly a hand slipped into hers and gave it a gentle squeeze before letting go again. Epimetheus! He and his brother had come into the grove to stand on either side of her.

"It was prophesied that she would open the box and release the trouble bubbles," Epimetheus told Zeus. "She recaptured them, though."

"Except for one," Pandora added. "The 'Hope' bubble." She sent Epimetheus a smile, grateful for his support. As they headed for the grove's exit, she and the others explained to Zeus all that had happened.

"Why make such a box in the first place?" Athena asked him as they neared the courtyard.

"It was a weapon. One that helped me win the war against the Titans," Zeus told them. "Those trouble bubbles made them lose their focus in battle, so we could capture and imprison them more easily."

Pandora felt Epimetheus and Prometheus tense at his mention of the war. The imprisonment of the Titans included their dad, of course.

"Is that why you invited us here? To get your box back?" Prometheus challenged.

"Partly," Zeus admitted. "After the war I lost track of it. I suspected that a Titan had it but wasn't sure who. Then your uncle wrote to me revealing he'd given it to you, and that Iapetus was angry with you for refusing to turn it over to him. Your uncle asked me to protect you. I agreed. But I didn't know you had brought the box to the Academy till it showed up on my desk last Monday."

Hearing this, Pandora felt sorry for the boys. It must've been hard for them not to give in to their dad's demand to give him the box. "Why *didn't* you let your dad have it?" she asked them.

"Because if our dad got the trouble bubbles, he might

start another Titan versus Olympian war," said Epimetheus. "He's never been able to accept that Zeus is the true and best ruler of Mount Olympus."

"No 'might' about it," Prometheus corrected him. "Dad threatened to do just that. Right before he told us he never wanted to see us again unless we were bringing him the box."

"How awful!" said Aphrodite. Pandora saw that all the girls' expressions had softened toward the boys.

"Now that you have the box again, will you destroy it?" Persephone asked Zeus.

He looked a little sad as he shook his head. "Once such trouble bubbles are created, they can never be destroyed. They'll always exist. So the best I can do now is to keep them safely imprisoned here in this box."

"We're sorry we didn't give you the box right away, as soon as we arrived at the Academy," Prometheus said to

Zeus. "Dad had us so confused by the horrible things he said about you that we decided to wait till we were sure you were the best choice to guard it."

Zeus gave the boys a low bow. "Well, on behalf of all of Mount Olympus, I thank you for your confidence. I will guard this box and keep it safely locked away forevermore."

"If you really want to thank us," Epimetheus blurted, "maybe you could release my brother from liver punishment."

"That's only fair," Pandora put in, hoping to help convince Zeus.

"Because the fire wasn't actually Prometheus's fault," added Athena.

Aphrodite nodded. "Yeah. He was under a bubble spell too."

"A 'thief' one," said Persephone.

"Consider it done," said Zeus. "Prometheus, I hereby shorten your punishment from an entire life of liver-eating to time served thus far."

"Yes!" Prometheus punched a jubilant fist in the air.

At the same time, the sound of flapping wings came from somewhere in the distance. Zeus's eagle-eyed eagle was returning to the forest now that it was no longer needed.

Zeus threw back his shoulders now, full of his old energy again. "Well, I'm off to restore things to normal down on Earth," he said. "As you noted, those mortals need fire—the controlled kind." He looked at the Titans. "Want to help me deliver it?" he asked.

Epimetheus and Prometheus nodded eagerly.

"Excellent! Afterward we can pay a visit to the Underworld and have a chat with your dad. We'll see if we can smooth things over between us all."

The boys seemed to brighten at this. Pandora knew it must mean that, deep down, they cared about their dad, in spite of their disagreement over the box.

As everyone began to go their separate ways, Epimetheus drew Pandora aside. To her surprise, he took both of her hands in his, his expression earnest.

"Well, I guess this is good-bye, at least for a while," he told her. "I didn't want to leave without saying—" He paused as if searching for the right word.

"Saying what?" She braced herself, unsure if he was going to say something kind or be critical.

"Just that I don't think you give yourself enough credit," he told her. "You're curious. And I think that's a good thing."

"But curiosity can also get you into trouble," Pandora said. "Like this week."

"Well, I *hope* you'll use yours in ways that don't from

now on," he said. This time they both grinned over his use of the word "hope."

He kept one of her hands in his as, together, they left the grove and headed for the courtyard. A warm feeling spread through her as they walked.

So this is what it feels like to hold hands with a boy you like, Pandora thought. It was nice. Really nice. And she did like Epimetheus, she realized. He *got* her.

It seemed hard to remember what she'd ever seen in Poseidon. Because now that she thought about it, that turquoise godboy was both drippy *and* dippy!

When they reached the courtyard, Epimetheus gave her fingers a light squeeze. His gray-green eyes smiled into her pale blue ones. "See you," he murmured.

"See you," she replied, smiling back at him.

Then he was stepping away. Pandora watched as

he, Prometheus, and Zeus prepared for takeoff in the Titan balloon.

"Woo-hoo!" Zeus shouted as they lifted off. He seemed as excited as a little kid to be going for a ride in it. Epimetheus sent her a big wave once they were airborne, and she waved back.

And just like that, he and his brother were gone from MOA.

14
Judges

"WE'D BETTER GET BACK TO OUR TABLES," SAID Athena. "Pythagoras and the others are making their rounds and will be judging soon."

"They're just now starting?" Pandora asked. She'd completely lost track of time and had thought the judging must already be over. Was it possible she still had a chance to keep from getting an incomplete?

Quickly she borrowed some art supplies from the goddessgirls, found an empty table, and began designing a poster. It was hard work, and she was doing it alone. Still, remembering Epimetheus's encouraging words, she felt buoyed to try her best. If she succeeded, her project would explain the events of the past week to all the students at MOA better than her own words could.

Before long she'd finished her poster and set out the hero statues that she and the Titans had made. Including the sooty one that had burned in the fire.

She finished in the nick of time, just as the judges arrived at her table. *Hoping* for a good outcome, she calmly explained her project to them, gesturing to each point on her poster in turn.

1. QUESTION - IS CURIOSITY A GOOD THING OR A BAD THING?

2. RESEARCH - I OPENED A MYSTERY BOX TO FIND OUT WHAT WAS INSIDE. OUR TEAM WENT TO EARTH TO ASK MORTALS WHAT THEY NEED.

3. HYPOTHESIS - CURIOSITY IS A GOOD THING. AND A BAD THING.

Her project went on to tell about the trouble bubbles, the Hero-ology fire, and how everything had gone awry. Then her conclusion wrapped things up.

6. CONCLUSION- CURIOSITY WAS HELPFUL IN FINDING OUT WHAT MORTALS NEED. BUT IT CAUSED TROUBLE WHEN I OPENED THE MYSTERY BOX. YET QUESTIONING THE UNKNOWN WILL ALWAYS BE A TEMPTATION TO THE CURIOUS, RIGHT? I *HOPE* SO!

• • •

That night in bed Pandora rolled onto her side. "You still awake?" she called softly toward Athena's bed across the room.

"Um-hmm," said Athena. "What's the matter? Can't sleep?"

"It's just that there's one thing I'm still curious about," said Pandora.

"No! You—curious? About what?" Athena replied in a teasing voice. It was almost the same thing she'd said to Pandora that day she'd first opened the mystery box.

Pandora smiled to herself, then spilled what was on her mind. "Epimetheus told me that an oracle had prophesied that a girl would open the box. Why me? Why was I able to break the lock on the box when no one else except Zeus could?"

"Who knows?" said Athena. "An oracle's prophecies

are never entirely clear. Maybe some mysteries just aren't meant to be solved."

Pandora nodded, forgetting that Athena couldn't see her in the dark. She was starting to doze off, when Athena murmured, "So did I do anything horribly embarrassing this week?"

"Are you sure you want to know?" asked Pandora.

"I think so," said Athena, though she didn't sound quite sure.

"Well, you kept getting lost in the halls," Pandora told her. "And you went to parties and giggled a lot. And you forgot how to spell and count. And I think you're going to have to ask for a new Spell-ology textscroll. Because you cut paper dolls out of your old one."

"Stop! You're kidding, right? Did I actually do all that?"

"Hey! Would I lie?" Pandora asked. "I'm not Pythagoras, you know."

They both giggled.

Just then there was a tap on their window. One of the magic breezes that delivered packages and letters to MOA was waiting outside.

"A message!" said Athena. She jumped up and went to open the window.

"So late?" asked Pandora, getting out of bed too.

"It's a box for you," said Athena, handing it to her. "And a letter. From Epimetheus."

"Awesome!" Excited now, Pandora ripped the letter open first. By the light of the moon shining through the window, she read it aloud:

DEAR PANDORA,

OUR DAD ISN'T SO MAD ANYMORE. ZEUS CALMED HIM DOWN. THEY

TALKED, AND MAYBE THEY'LL BE FRIENDS SOMEDAY. WE'RE GOING TO GO LIVE WITH OUR UNCLE AGAIN AND CAN VISIT DAD NOW AND THEN.

WELL, I <u>HOPE</u> YOU WRITE BACK.

MEANWHILE, I SENT YOU SOMETHING TO REMEMBER ME BY. A BOX. AND DON'T WORRY—IT'S PERFECTLY SAFE TO OPEN IT.

EPIMETHEUS

Pandora set his letter aside and shook the box. "It sounds sloshy. I wonder what it could be?"

"Only one way to find out," said Athena.

Swiftly Pandora unwrapped the box, which was about ten inches tall. Though she was curious about what it contained, she paused before she peeked inside. Epimetheus had said it was safe to open, and she trusted him to tell the truth. Still, she couldn't help being a bit nervous after what had happened when she'd opened his other box.

She took a deep breath. "Well, here goes!" She opened the box and pulled out . . .

"A bottle?" she said in surprise. She unscrewed its lid and looked inside. She sniffed. Then she read the label and started to laugh.

"What's so funny?" Athena asked.

Pandora held the bottle up so Athena could read the label. "It's full of . . ." Pandora was laughing so hard, she could hardly get the words out. "Of *bubble* bath."

They both began to giggle like crazy, falling onto the floor, where they giggled some more.

When their laughter finally slowed, Pandora set the bottle on the shelf above her desk. Right next to her Science-ology textscroll. Just a few hours ago she'd erased the *P* and *P* letters she'd doodled on it before and replaced them with the intertwined letters *P* and *E*.

She had a new crush now. One who sent her funny presents and who *got* her. One who even liked that she was curious!

The following Monday, another, more official-looking letter arrived for Pandora during lunch. Everyone turned to look as a magic breeze whirled it across the cafeteria to plop it onto her table.

Her jaw dropped and her eyes got big when she read

it. She immediately jumped up and ran over to the popular table.

"Guess what?" she told Athena. "My Science-ology fair project won first prize? Lunch with all three judges? Including Pythagoras?" As usual, her excitement was making her speak in questions.

"Wow! Epic news!" said a voice behind her. Pheme had followed her and overheard. Now she dashed off, running from table to table to spread the word.

But Pandora didn't mind a bit. She'd proven her scientific smarts to the judges, and thanks to Pheme, soon the whole Academy would know about it. Including Poseidon. Ha!

"Congratulations," Athena told Pandora, sounding happy for her. "I'm glad you won. When's the lunch?"

"Today. A chariot's coming for us in an hour."

"Us?"

"Yeah. I get to choose someone to come with me. Don't you want to go to lunch with Pythagoras, Aristotle, Hippocrates, and me?" Pandora asked her.

Athena's enthusiastic squeal practically burst everyone's eardrums. "You're taking *me*?"

At Pandora's nod Athena jumped from her chair and bounced on her toes. "You are the best roomie ever!" She gave Pandora a huge hug.

Pandora grinned at her. "C'mon. Let's get going. There's a lot we can learn from those scientists. But our questions aren't going to ask themselves!"